D0930082

TIGERS ARE BETTER-LOOKING

BY THE SAME AUTHOR

WIDE SARGASSO SEA
GOOD MORNING, MIDNIGHT
VOYAGE IN THE DARK
AFTER LEAVING MR MACKENZIE

TIGERS ARE BETTER-LOOKING
with a selection from
THE LEFT BANK

❧

stories by

JEAN RHYS

HARPER & ROW, PUBLISHERS

NEW YORK, EVANSTON, SAN FRANCISCO, LONDON

This book was first published in 1968 by Andre Deutsch Limited.

'Till September Petronella,' 'The Day they Burned the Books,' 'Tigers Are Better-Looking' and 'Let them Call it Jazz' were first published in *The London Magazine* (copyright © Jean Rhys, 1960, 1960, 1962 and 1962); 'The Sound of the River' and 'The Lotus' were first published in *Art and Literature* numbers 9 and 11 (copyright © Jean Rhys, 1966 and 1967); 'Outside the Machine' was first published in *Winter's Tales,* Macmillan (copyright © Jean Rhys, 1960); 'A Solid House' was first published in *Voices,* Michael Joseph (copyright © Jean Rhys, 1963).

The stories from *The Left Bank* were first published by Jonathan Cape (London) and Harper & Brothers (New York) in 1927.

FIRST U.S. EDITION

ISBN: 0-06-013561-1

LIBRARY OF CONGRESS CATALOG CARD NUMBER: 72-9175

Contents

TIGERS ARE BETTER-LOOKING

Till September Petronella 11
The Day they Burned the Books 40
Let them Call it Jazz 47
Tigers Are Better-Looking 68
Outside the Machine 83
The Lotus 107
A Solid House 120
The Sound of the River 138

THE LEFT BANK

Preface to a Selection of Stories from *The Left Bank* 147
Illusion 151
From a French Prison 156
Mannequin 160
Tea with an Artist 167
Mixing Cocktails 173
Again the Antilles 177
Hunger 181
La Grosse Fifi 185
Vienne 202

TIGERS ARE BETTER-LOOKING

Till September Petronella

THERE was a barrel organ playing at the corner of Torrington Square. It played *Destiny* and *La Paloma* and *Le Rêve Passe*, all tunes I liked, and the wind was warm and kind not spiteful, which doesn't often happen in London. I packed the striped dress that Estelle had helped me to choose, and the cheap white one that fitted well, and my best underclothes, feeling very happy while I was packing. A bit of a change, for that had not been one of my lucky summers.

I would tell myself it was the colour of the carpet or something about my room which was depressing me, but it wasn't that. And it wasn't anything to do with money either. I was making nearly five pounds a week – very good for me, and different from when I first started, when I was walking round trying to get work. *No* Hawkers, *No* Models, some of them put up, and you stand there, your hands cold and clammy, afraid to ring the bell. But I had got past that stage; this depression had nothing to do with money.

I often wished I was like Estelle, this French girl who lived in the big room on the ground floor. She had everything so cut-and-dried, she walked the tightrope so beautifully, not even knowing she was walking it. I'd think about the talks we had, and her clothes and her scent and the way she did her hair, and that when I went into her room it didn't seem like a Bloomsbury bed-sitting room – and when it comes to Bloomsbury bed-sitting rooms I know what I'm talking about. No, it was like a room out of one of those long, romantic novels, six hundred and fifty pages of small print, translated from French or German or Hungarian or something – because few of the English ones have the exact feeling I mean. And you read one page of it or even one phrase of it, and then you gobble up all the rest and go about in a dream for weeks afterwards, for months afterwards – perhaps all your life, who knows? – surrounded by those six hundred and fifty pages, the houses, the streets, the snow, the river, the roses, the girls, the sun, the ladies' dresses and the gentlemen's voices, the old, wicked, hard-hearted women and the old, sad women, the waltz music, everything. What is not there you put in afterwards, for it is alive, this book, and it grows in your head. 'The house I was living in when I read that book,' you think, or 'This colour reminds me of that book.'

It was after Estelle left, telling me she was going to Paris and wasn't sure whether she was coming back, that I struck a bad patch. Several of the people I was sitting to left London in June, but, instead of arranging for more work, I took long walks, zigzag, always the same way – Euston Road, Hampstead Road, Camden Town – though I hated those streets, which were like a grey nightmare in the sun. You saw so many old women, or women who seemed old, peering at the vegetables in the Camden Town market, looking at you with hatred, or blankly, as though they had forgotten your language, and talked another one. 'My God,' I would think, 'I hope I never live to be old. Anyway, however old I get, I'll never let my hair go grey. I'll dye it black, red, any colour you like, but I'll never let it go grey. I hate grey too much.' Coming back from one of these walks the thought came to me suddenly, like a revelation, that I could kill myself any time I liked and so end it. After that I put a better face on things.

When Marston wrote and I told the landlord I was going away for a fortnight, he said 'So there's a good time coming for the ladies, is there? – a good time coming for the girls? About time too.'

Marston said, 'You seem very perky, my dear. I hardly recognized you.'

I looked along the platform, but Julian had not come to meet me. There was only Marston, his long, white face and his pale-blue eyes, smiling.

'What a gigantic suitcase,' he said. 'I have my motorbike here, but I suppose I'd better leave it. We'll take a cab.'

It was getting dark when we reached the cottage, which stood by itself on rising ground. There were two elm trees in a field near the verandah, but the country looked bare, with low, grassy hills.

As we walked up the path through the garden I could hear Julian laughing and a girl talking, her voice very high and excited, though she put on a calm, haughty expression as we came into the room. Her dress was red, and she wore several coloured glass bangles which tinkled when she moved.

Marston said, 'This is Frankie. You've met the great Julian, of course.'

Well, I knew Frankie Morell by sight, but as she didn't say anything about it I didn't either. We smiled at each other cautiously, falsely.

The table was laid for four people. The room looked comfortable but there were no flowers. I had expected that they would have it full of flowers. However, there were some sprays of honeysuckle in a green jug in my bedroom and

Marston, standing in the doorway, said, 'I walked miles to get you that honeysuckle this morning. I thought about you all the time I was picking it.'

'Don't be long,' he said. 'We're all very hungry.'

We ate ham and salad and drank perry. It went to my head a bit. Julian talked about his job which he seemed to dislike. He was the music critic of one of the daily papers. 'It's a scandal. One's forced to down the right people and praise the wrong people.'

'Forced?' said Marston.

'Well, they drop very strong hints.'

'I'll take the plates away,' Frankie told me. 'You can start tomorrow. Not one of the local women will do a thing for us. We've only been here a fortnight, but they've got up a hate you wouldn't believe. Julian says he almost faints when he thinks of it. I say, why think of it?'

When she came back she turned the lamp out. Down there it was very still. The two trees outside did not move, or the moon.

Julian lay on the sofa and I was looking at his face and his hair when Marston put his arms round me and kissed me. But I watched Julian and listened to him whistling – stopping, laughing, beginning again.

'What was that music?' I said, and Frankie answered in a patronizing voice, '*Tristan*, second act duet.'

'I've never been to that opera.'

I had never been to any opera. All the same, I could imagine it. I could imagine myself in a box, wearing a moonlight-blue dress and silver shoes, and when the lights went up everybody asking, 'Who's that lovely girl in that box?' But it must happen quickly or it will be too late.

Marston squeezed my hand. 'Very fine performance, Julian,' he said, 'very fine. Now forgive me, my dears, I must leave you. All this emotion – '

Julian lighted the lamp, took a book from the shelf and began to read.

Frankie blew on the nails of one hand and polished them on the edge of the other. Her nails were nice – of course, you could get a manicure for a bob then – but her hands were large and too white for her face. 'I've seen you at the Apple Tree, surely.' The Apple Tree was a night club in Greek Street.

'Oh yes, often.'

'But you've cut your hair. I wanted to cut mine, but Julian asked me not to. He begged me not to. Didn't you, Julian?'

Julian did not answer.

'He said he'd lose his strength if I cut my hair.'

Julian turned over a page and went on reading.

'This isn't a bad spot, is it?' Frankie said. 'Not one of those places where the ceiling's on top of your head and you've got to walk four miles in the dark to the lavatory. There are two other bedrooms besides the one Marston gave you. Come and have a look at them. You can change over if you want to. We'll never tear Julian away from his book. It's about the biological inferiority of women. That's what you told me, Julian, isn't it?'

'Oh, *go* away,' Julian said.

We ended up in her room, where she produced some head and figure studies, photographs.

'Do you like these? Do you know this man? He says I'm the best model he's ever had. He says I'm far and away the best model in London.'

'Beautiful. Lovely photographs.'

But Frankie, sitting on the big bed, said, 'Aren't people swine? Julian says I never think. He's wrong, sometimes I think quite a lot. The other day I spent a long time trying to decide which were worse – men or women.'

'I wonder.'

'Women are worse.'

She had long, calm black hair, drawn away from her face and hanging smoothly almost to her waist, and a calm, clear little voice and a calm, haughty expression.

'They'll kick your face to bits if you let them. And shriek with laughter at the damage. But I'm not going to let them – oh no . . . Marston's always talking about you,' she said. 'He's very fond of you, poor old Marston. Do you know that picture as you go into his studio – in the entrance place? What's he say it is?'

'The Apotheosis of Lust.'

'Yes, the Apotheosis of Lust. I have to laugh when I think of that, for some reason. Poor old Andy Marston . . . But I don't know why I should say "Poor old Andy Marston". He'll always have one penny to tinkle against another. His family's very wealthy, you know.'

'He makes me go cold.'

I thought, 'Why did I say that?' Because I like Marston.

'So that's how you feel about him, is it?' She seemed pleased, as if she had heard something she wanted to hear, had been waiting to hear.

'Are you tired?' Marston said.

I was looking out of the bedroom window at some sheep feeding in the field where the elm trees grew.

'A bit,' I said. 'A bit very.'

His mouth drooped, disappointed.

'Oh, Marston, thank you for asking me down here. It's so lovely to get away from London; it's like a dream.'

'A dream, my God! However, when it comes to dreams, why shouldn't they be pleasant?'

He sat down on the windowsill.

'The great Julian's not so bad, is he?'

'Why do you call him the great Julian? As if you were gibing at him.'

'Gibing at him? Good Lord, far be it from me to gibe at him. He *is* the great Julian. He's going to be very important, so far as an English musician can be important. He's horribly conceited, though. Not about his music, of course – he's conceited about his personal charm. I can't think why. He's a very ordinary type really. You see that nose and mouth and hear that voice all over the place. You rather dislike him, don't you?'

'Do I?'

'Of course you do. Have you forgotten how annoyed you were when I told you that he'd have to *see* a female before he could consent to live at close quarters with her for two weeks? You were quite spirited about it, I thought. Don't say that was only a flash in the pan, you poor devil of a female, female, female, in a country where females are only tolerated at best! What's going to become of you, Miss Petronella Gray, living in a bed-sitting room in Torrington Square, with no money, no background and no nous? . . . Is Petronella your real name?'

'Yes.'

'You worry me, whatever your name is. I bet it isn't Gray.'

I thought, 'What does it matter? If you knew how bloody my home was you wouldn't be surprised that I wanted to change my name and forget all about it.'

I said, not looking at him, 'I was called after my grandmother – Julia Petronella.'

'Oh, you've got a grandmother, have you? Fancy that! Now, for Heaven's sake don't put on that expression. Take my advice and grow another skin or two and sharpen your claws before it's too late. *Before it's too late*, mark those words. If you don't, you're going to have a hell of a time.'

'So that I long for death?'

He looked startled. 'Why do you say that?'

'It was only the first thing that came into my head from nowhere. I was joking.'

When he did not answer, 'Well, good night,' I said. 'Sleep tight.'

'I shan't sleep,' he said. 'I shall probably have to listen to those two for quite a time yet. When they're amorous they're noisy and when they fight it's worse. She goes for him with a pen-knife. Mind you, she only does that because he likes it, but her good nature is a pretence. She's a bitch really. Shut your door and you won't hear anything. Will you be sad tomorrow?'

'Of course not.'

'Don't look as if you'd lost a shilling and found sixpence then,' he said, and went out.

That's the way they always talk. 'You look as if you'd lost a shilling and found sixpence,' they say; 'You look very perky, I hardly recognized you,' they say; '*Look gay*,' they say. 'My dear Petronella, I have an entirely new idea of you. I'm going to paint you out in the opulent square. So can you wear something gay tomorrow afternoon? Not one of those drab affairs you usually clothe yourself in. Gay – do you know the meaning of the word? Think about it, it's very important.'

The things you remember. . . .

Once, left alone in a very ornate studio, I went up to a plaster cast – the head of a man, one of those Greek heads – and kissed it, because it was so beautiful. Its mouth felt warm, not cold. It was smiling. When I kissed it the room went dead silent and I was frightened. I told Estelle about this one day. 'Does that sound mad?' She didn't laugh. She said, 'Who hasn't kissed a picture or a photograph and suddenly been frightened?'

The music Julian had been whistling was tormenting me. That, and the blind eyes of the plaster cast, and the way the sun shone on the black iron bedstead in my room in Torrington

Square on fine days. The bars of the bedstead grin at me. Sometimes I count the knobs on the chest of drawers three times over. 'One of those drab affairs! . . .'

I began to talk to Julian in my head. Was it to Julian? 'I'm not like that. I'm not at all like that. They're trying to make me like that, but I'm not like that.'

After a while I took a pencil and paper and wrote, 'I love Julian. Julian, I kissed you once, but you didn't know.'

I folded the paper several times and hid it under some clothes in my suitcase. Then I went to bed and slept at once.

Where our path joined the main road there were some cottages. As Marston and I came back from our walk next morning we passed two women in their gardens, which were full of lupins and poppies. They looked at us sullenly, as though they disliked us. When Marston said 'Good morning', they did not answer.

'Surly, priggish brutes,' he muttered, 'but that's how they are.'

The grass round our cottage was long and trampled in places. There were no flowers.

'They're back,' Marston said. 'There's the motorbike.'

They came out on to the verandah, very spruce; Frankie in her red frock with her hair tied up in a red and blue handkerchief, Julian wearing a brown coat over a blue shirt and shabby grey trousers like Marston's. Very gay, I thought. (*Gay – do you know the meaning of the word?*)

'What's the matter with you, Marston?' Julian said. 'You look frightful.'

'You do seem a bit upset,' Frankie said. 'What happened? Do tell.'

'Don't tell her anything,' said Marston. 'I'm going to dress up too. Why should I be the only one in this resplendent assembly with a torn shirt and stained bags? Wait till you see what I've got – and I don't mean what you mean.'

'Let's get the food ready,' Frankie said to me.

The kitchen table was covered with things they had brought from Cheltenham, and there were several bottles of white wine cooling in a bucket of water in the corner.

'What have you done to Marston?'

'Nothing. What on earth do you mean?'

Nothing had happened. We were sitting under a tree, looking at a field of corn, and Marston put his head in my lap and then a man came along and yelled at us. I said, 'What do you think we're doing to your corn? Can't we even look at your corn?' But Marston only mumbled, 'I'm fearfully sorry. I'm dreadfully sorry,' and so on. And then we went walking along the main road in the sun, not talking much because I was hating him.

'Nothing happened,' I said.

'Oh well, it's a pity, because Julian's in a bad mood today. However, don't take any notice of him. Don't start a row whatever you do; just smooth it over.'

'Look at the lovely bit of steak I got,' she said. 'Marston says he can't touch any meat except cold ham, I ask you, and he does the cooking. Cold ham and risotto, risotto and cold ham. And curried eggs. That's what we've been living on ever since we came down here.'

When we went in with the food they had finished a bottle of wine. Julian said, 'Here's luck to the ruddy citizens I saw this morning. May they be flourishing and producing offspring exactly like themselves, but far, far worse, long after we are all in our dishonoured graves.'

Marston was now wearing black silk pyjamas with a pattern of red and green dragons. His long, thin neck and sad face looked extraordinary above this get-up. Frankie and I glanced at each other and giggled. Julian scowled at me.

Marston went over to the mirror. 'Never mind,' he said softly to his reflection, 'never mind, never mind.'

'It's ham and salad again,' Frankie said. 'But I've got some prunes.'

The table was near the window. A hot, white glare shone in our eyes. We tried pulling the blinds down, but one got stuck and we went on eating in the glare.

Then Frankie talked about the steak again. 'You must have your first bite tonight, Marston.'

'It won't be my first bite,' Marston said. 'I've been persuaded to taste beef before.'

'Oh, you never told me that. No likee?'

'I thought it would taste like sweat,' Marston said, 'and it did.'

Frankie looked annoyed. 'The trouble with you people is that you try to put other people off just because you don't fancy a thing. If you'd just not like it and leave it at that, but you don't *rest* till you've put everybody else off.'

'Oh God, let's get tight,' Julian said. 'There are bottles and bottles of wine in the kitchen. Cooling, I hope.'

'We'll get them,' Frankie said, 'we'll get them.'

Frankie sat on the kitchen table. 'I think Julian's spoiling for a fight. Let him calm down a bit. . . . You're staving Marston off, aren't you? And he doesn't like it; he's very disconsolate. You've got to be careful of these people, they can be as hard as nails.'

Far away a dog barked, a cock crew, somebody was sawing wood. I hardly noticed what she had said because again it came, that feeling of happiness, the fish-in-water feeling, so that I couldn't even remember having been unhappy.

Frankie started on a long story about a man called Petersen

who had written a play about Northern gods and goddesses and Yggdrasil.

'I thought Yggdrasil was a girl, but it seems it's a tree.'

Marston and Julian and all that lot had taken Petersen up, she said. They used to ask him out and make him drunk. Then he would take his clothes off and dance about and if he did not do it somebody would be sure to say, 'What's the matter? Why don't you perform?' But as soon as he got really sordid they had dropped him like a hot brick. He simply disappeared.

'I met an old boy who knew him and asked what had happened. The old boy said, "A gigantic maw has swallowed Petersen . . ." Maw, what a word! It reminds me of Julian's mother – she's a maw if you like. Well, I'd better take these bottles along now.'

So we took the four bottles out of the bucket and went back into the sitting-room. It was still hot and glaring, but not quite so bad as it had been.

'Now it's my turn to make a speech,' said Marston. 'But you must drink, pretty creatures, drink.' He filled our glasses and I drank mine quickly. He filled it up again.

'My speech,' he said, 'my speech. . . . Let's drink to afternoon, the best of all times. Cruel morning is past, fearful, unpredictable, lonely night is yet to come. Here's to heart-rending afternoon . . . I will now recite a poem. It's hackneyed and pawed about, like so many other things, but beautiful. "C'est bien la pire peine de ne savoir pourquoi – " '

He stopped and began to cry. We all looked at him. Nobody laughed; nobody knew what to say. I felt shut in by the glare.

Marston blew his nose, wiped his eyes and gabbled on: ' "Pourquoi, sans amour et sans haine, Mon coeur a tant de peine. . . ." '

' "Sans amour" is right,' Julian said, staring at me. I looked back into his eyes.

' "But for loving, why, you would not, Sweet," ' Marston went on, ' "Though we prayed you, Paid you, brayed you In a mortar – for you could not, Sweet." '

'The motorbike was altogether a bit of luck,' Frankie said. 'Julian had a fight with a man on the bus going in. I thought he'd have a fit.'

'Fight?' Julian said. 'I never fight. I'm frightened.'

He was still staring at me.

'Well then, you were very rude.'

'I'm never rude, either,' Julian said. 'I'm far too frightened ever to be rude. I suffer in silence.'

'I shouldn't do that if I were you,' I said. The wine was making me giddy. So was the glare, and the way he was looking at me

'What's this young creature up to?' he said. 'I can't quite make her out.'

'Ruddy respectable citizens never can.'

'Ha-hah,' Frankie said. 'One in the eye for you, Julian. You're always going on about respectable people, but you know *you* are respectable, whatever you say and whatever you do, and you'll be respectable till you die, however you die, and that way you miss something, believe it or not.'

'You keep out of this, Phoenician,' Julian said. 'You've got nothing to say. Retire under the table, because that's where I like you best.'

Frankie crawled under the table. She darted her head out now and again, pretending to bite his legs, and every time she did that he would shiver and scream.

'Oh, come on out,' he said at last. 'It's too hot for these antics.'

Frankie crawled out again, very pleased with herself, went to the mirror and arranged the handkerchief round her hair. 'Am I really like a Phoenician?'

'Of course you are. A Phoenician from Cornwall, England. Direct descent, I should say.'

'And what's she?' Frankie said. Her eyes looked quite different, like snake's eyes. We all looked quite different – it's funny what drink does.

'That's very obvious too,' Julian said.

'All right, why don't you come straight out with it?' I said. 'Or are you frightened?'

'Sometimes words fail.'

Marston waved his arms about. 'Julian, you stop this. I won't have it.'

'You fool,' Julian said, 'you fool. Can't you see she's fifth-rate. Can't you see?'

'You ghastly cross between a barmaid and a chorus-girl,' he said; 'You female spider,' he said; 'You've been laughing at him for weeks,' he said, 'jeering at him, sniggering at him. Stopping him from working – the best painter in this damnable island, the only one in my opinion. And then when I try to get him away from you, of course you follow him down here.'

'That's not it at all,' Marston said. 'You're not being fair to the girl. You don't understand her a bit.'

'She doesn't care,' Julian said. 'Look at her – she's giggling her stupid head off.'

'Well, what are you to do when you come up against a mutual admiration society?' I said.

'You're letting your jealousy run away with you,' said Marston.

'Jealousy?' Julian said. 'Jealousy!' He was unrecognizable. His beautiful eyes were little, mean pits and you looked down them into nothingness.

'Jealous of what?' he shrieked. 'Why, do you know that she told Frankie last night that she can't bear you and that the only reason she has anything to do with you is because she wants money. What do you think of that? Does that open your eyes?'

'Now, *Julian*!' Frankie's voice was as loud and high as his. 'You'd no right to repeat that. You promised you wouldn't and anyway you've exaggerated it. It's all very well for you to talk about how inferior women are, but you get more like your horrible mother every moment.'

'You do,' Marston said, quite calm now. 'Julian, you really do.'

'Do you know what all this is about?' Frankie said, nodding at Julian. 'It's because he doesn't want me to go back to London with him. He wants me to go and be patronized and educated by his detestable mother in her dreary house in the dreary country, who will then say that the case is hopeless. Wasn't she a good sort and a saint to try? But the girl is *quite impossible.* Do you think I don't know that trick? It's as old as the hills.

'You're mean,' she said to Julian, 'and you hate girls really. Don't imagine I don't see through you. You're trying to get me down. But you won't do it. If you think you're the only man in the world who's fond of me *or* that I'm a goddamned fool, you're making the hell of a big mistake, you and your mother.'

She plucked a hairpin from her hair, bent it into the shape of pince-nez and went on in a mincing voice, 'Do Ay understend you tew say thet *may* sonn – ' she placed the pince-nez on her nose and looked over it sourly ' – with *one* connection – '

'Damn you,' said Julian, 'damn you, damn you.'

'Now they're off,' Marston said placidly. 'Drinking on a hot afternoon is a mistake. The pen-knife will be out in a minute . . . Don't go. Stay and watch the fun. My money on Frankie every time.'

But I went into the bedroom and shut the door. I could hear them wrangling and Marston, very calm and superior, putting in a word now and again. Then nothing. They had gone on to the verandah.

I got the letter I had written and tore it very carefully into four pieces. I spat on each piece. I opened the door – there was not a sign of them. I took the pieces of paper to the lavatory, emptied them in and pulled the plug. As soon as I heard the water gushing I felt better.

The door of the kitchen was open and I saw that there was another path leading to the main road.

And there I was, walking along, not thinking of anything, my eyes fixed on the ground. I walked a long way like that, not looking up, though I passed several people. At last I came to a sign-post. I was on the Cirencester road. Something about the word 'miles' written made me feel very tired.

A little farther on the wall on one side of the road was low. It was the same wall on which Marston and I had sat that morning, and he had said, 'Do you think we could rest here or will the very stones rise up against us?' I looked round and there was nobody in sight, so I stepped over it and sat down in the shade. It was pretty country, but bare. The white, glaring look was still in the sky.

Close by there was a dove cooing. 'Coo away, dove,' I thought. 'It's no use, no use, still coo away, coo away.'

After a while the dazed feeling, as if somebody had hit me on the head, began to go. I thought 'Cirencester – and then a train to London. It's as easy as that.'

Then I realized that I had left my handbag and money, as well as everything else, in the bedroom at the cottage, but imagining walking back there made me feel so tired that I could hardly put one foot in front of the other.

I got over the wall. A car that was coming along slowed down and stopped and the man driving it said, 'Want a lift?'

I went up to the car.

'Where do you want to go?'

'I want to go to London.'

'To London? Well, I can't take you as far as that, but I can get you into Cirencester to catch a train if you like.'

I said anxiously, 'Yes – but I must go back first to the place where I've been staying. It's not far.'

'Haven't time for that. I've got an appointment. I'm late already and I mustn't miss it. Tell you what – come along with me. If you'll wait till I've done I can take you to fetch your things.'

I got into the car. As soon as I touched him I felt comforted. Some men are like that.

'Well, you look as if you'd lost a shilling and found sixpence.'

Again I had to laugh.

'That's better. Never does any good to be down in the mouth.'

'We're nearly in Cirencester now,' he said after a while. 'I've got to see a lot of people. This is market day and I'm a farmer. I'll take you to a nice quiet place where you can have a cup of tea while you're waiting.'

He drove to a pub in a narrow street. 'This way in.' I followed him into the bar.

'Good afternoon, Mrs Strickland. Lovely day, isn't it? Will you give my friend a cup of tea while I'm away, and make her comfortable? She's very tired.'

'I will, certainly,' Mrs Strickland said, with a swift glance up and down. 'I expect the young lady would like a nice wash too, wouldn't she?' She was dark and nicely got up, but her voice had a tinny sound.

'Oh, I would.'

I looked down at my crumpled white dress. I touched my face for I knew there must be a red mark where I had lain with it pressed against the ground.

'See you later,' the farmer said.

There were brightly polished taps in the ladies' room and a

very clean red and black tiled floor. I washed my hands, tried to smooth my dress, and powdered my face – Poudre Nildé basanée – but I did it without looking in the glass.

Tea and cakes were laid in a small, dark, stuffy room. There were three pictures of Lady Hamilton, Johnny Walker advertisements, china bulldogs wearing sailor caps and two calendars. One said January 9th, but the other was right – July 28th, 1914. . . .

'Well, here I am.' He sat heavily down beside me. 'Did Mrs Strickland look after you all right?'

'Very well.'

'Oh, she's a good sort, she's a nice woman. She's known me a long time. Of course, you haven't, have you? But everything's got to have a start.'

Then he said he hadn't done so badly that afternoon and stretched out his legs, looking pleased, looking happy as the day is long.

'What were you thinking about when I came in? You nearly jumped out of your skin.'

'I was thinking about the time.'

'About the time? Oh, don't worry about that. There's plenty of time.'

He produced a large silver case, took out a cigar and lighted it, long and slow. 'Plenty of time,' he said. 'Dark in here, isn't it? So you live in London, do you?'

'Yes.'

'I've often thought I'd like to know a nice girl up in London.'

His eyes were fixed on Lady Hamilton and I knew he was imagining a really lovely girl – all curves, curls, heart and hidden claws. He swallowed, then put his hand over mine.

'I'd like to feel that when I go up to Town there's a friend I could see and have a good time with. You know. And I could give her a good time too. By God, I could. I know what women like.'

'You do?'

'Yes, I do. They like a bit of loving, that's what they like, isn't it? A bit of loving. All women like that. They like it dressed up sometimes – and sometimes not, it all depends. You have to know, and I know. I just know.'

'You've nothing more to learn, have you?'

'Not in that way I haven't. And they like pretty dresses and bottles of scent, and bracelets with blue stones in them. I know. Well, what about it?' he said, but as if he were joking.

I looked away from him at the calendar and did not answer, making my face blank.

'What about it?' he repeated.

'It's nice of you to say you want to see me again – very polite.'

He laughed. 'You think I'm being polite, do you? Well, perhaps – perhaps not. No harm in asking, was there? No offence meant – or taken, I hope. It's all right. I'll take you to get your things and catch your train – and we'll have a bottle of something good before we start off. It won't hurt you. It's bad stuff hurts you, not good stuff. You haven't found that out yet, but you will. Mrs Strickland has some good stuff, I can tell you – good enough for me, and I want the best.'

So we had a bottle of Clicquot in the bar.

He said, 'It puts some life into you, doesn't it?'

It did too. I wasn't feeling tired when we left the pub, nor even sad.

'Well,' he said as we got into the car, 'you've got to tell me where to drive to. And you don't happen to know a little song, do you?'

'That was very pretty,' he said when I stopped. 'You've got a very pretty voice indeed. Give us some more.'

But we were getting near the cottage and I didn't finish the next song because I was nervous and worried that I wouldn't be able to tell him the right turning.

At the foot of the path I thought, 'The champagne worked all right.'

He got out of the car and came with me. When we reached the gate leading into the garden he stood by my side without speaking.

They were on the verandah. We could hear their voices clearly.

'Listen, fool,' Julian was saying, 'listen, half-wit. What I said yesterday has nothing to do with what I say today or what I shall say tomorrow. Why should it?'

'That's what you think,' Frankie said obstinately. 'I don't agree with you. It might have something to do with it whether you like it or not.'

'Oh, stop arguing, you two,' Marston said. 'It's all very well for you, Julian, but I'm worried about that girl. I'm responsible. She looked so damned miserable. Supposing she's gone and made away with herself. I shall feel awful. Besides, probably I shall be held up to every kind of scorn and obloquy – as usual. And though it's all your fault you'll escape scot-free – also as usual.'

'Are those your friends?' the farmer asked.

'Well, they're my friends in a way . . . I have to go in to get my things. It won't take me long.'

Julian said, 'I think, I rather think, Marston, that I hear a female pipe down there. You can lay your fears away. She's not the sort to kill herself. I told you that.'

'Who's that?' the farmer said.

'That's Mr Oakes, one of my hosts.'

'Oh, is it? I don't like the sound of him. I don't like the sound of any of them. Shall I come with you?'

'No, don't. I won't be long.'

I went round by the kitchen into my room, walking very softly. I changed into my dark dress and then began to throw my things into the suitcase. I did all this as quickly as I could, but before I had finished Marston came in, still wearing his black pyjamas crawling with dragons.

'Who were you talking to outside?'

'Oh, that's a man I met. He's going to drive me to Cirencester to catch the London train.'

'You're not offended, are you?'

'Not a bit. Why should I be?'

'Of course, the great Julian can be so difficult,' he murmured. 'But don't think I didn't stick up for you, because I did. I said to him, "It's all very well for you to be rude to a girl I bring down, but what about your loathly Frankie, whom you inflict upon me day after day and week after week and I never say a word? I'm never even sharp to her – " What are you smiling at?'

'The idea of your being sharp to Frankie.'

'The horrid little creature!' Marston said excitedly, 'the unspeakable bitch! But the day will come when Julian will find her out and he'll run to me for sympathy. I'll not give it him. Not after this. . . . Cheer up,' he said. 'The world is big. There's hope.'

'Of course.' But suddenly I saw the women's long, scowling faces over their lupins and their poppies, and my room in Torrington Square and the iron bars of my bedstead, and I thought, 'Not for me.'

'It may all be necessary,' he said, as if he were talking to himself. 'One has to get an entirely different set of values to be any good.'

I said, 'Do you think I could go out through the window? I don't want to meet them.'

'I'll come to the car with you. What's this man like?'

'Well, he's a bit like the man this morning, and he says he doesn't care for the sound of you.'

'Then I think I won't come. Go through the window and I'll hand your suitcase to you.'

He leaned out and said, 'See you in September, Petronella. I'll be back in September.'

I looked up at him. 'All right. Same old address.'

The farmer said, 'I was coming in after you. You're well rid of that lot – never did like that sort. Too many of them about.'

'They're all right.'

'Well, tune up,' he said, and I sang 'Mr Brown, Mr Brown, Had a violin, Went around, went around, With his violin.' I sang all the way to Cirencester.

At the station he gave me my ticket and a box of chocolates.

'I bought these for you this afternoon, but I forgot them. Better hurry – there's not much time.'

'Fare you well,' he said. 'That's what they say in Norfolk, where I come from.'

'Good-bye.'

'No, say fare you well.'

'Fare you well.'

The train started.

'This is very nice,' I thought, 'my first-class carriage,' and had a long look at myself in the glass for the first time since it had happened. 'Never mind,' I said, and remembered Marston saying 'Never mind, never mind.'

'Don't look so down in the mouth, my girl,' I said to myself. '*Look gay.*'

'Cheer up,' I said, and kissed myself in the cool glass. I stood with my forehead against it and watched my face clouding gradually, then turned because I felt as if someone was staring at me, but it was only the girl on the cover of the chocolate-box. She had slanting green eyes, but they were too close together, and she had a white, square, smug face that didn't go with her slanting eyes. 'I bet you could be a rotten, respectable, sneering bitch too, with a face like that, if you had the chance,' I told her.

The train got into Paddington just before ten. As soon as I was on the platform I remembered the chocolates, but I didn't go back for them. 'Somebody will find you, somebody will look after you, you rotten, sneering, stupid, tight-mouthed bitch,' I thought.

London always smells the same. 'Frowsty,' you think, 'but I'm glad to be back.' And just for a while it bears you up. 'Anything's round the corner,' you think. But long before you get round the corner it lets you drop.

I decided that I'd walk for a bit with the suitcase and get tired and then perhaps I'd sleep. But at the corner of Marylebone Road and Edgware Road my arm was stiff and I put down the suitcase and waved at a taxi standing by the kerb.

'Sorry, miss,' the driver said, 'this gentleman was first.'

The young man smiled. 'It's all right. You have it.'

'You have it,' he said. The other one said, 'Want a lift?'

'I can get the next one. I'm not in any hurry.'

'Nor am I.'

The taxi-driver moved impatiently.

'Well, don't let's hesitate any longer,' the young man said, 'or we'll lose our taximeter-cab. Get in – I can easily drop you wherever you're going.'

'Go along Edgware Road,' he said to the driver. 'I'll tell you where in a minute.'

The taxi started.

'Where to?'

'Torrington Square.'

The house would be waiting for me. 'When I pass Estelle's door,' I thought, 'there'll be no smell of scent now.' Then I was back in my small room on the top floor, listening to the church clock chiming every quarter-hour. 'There's a good time coming for the ladies. There's a good time coming for the girls. . . .'

I said, 'Wait a minute. I don't want to go to Torrington Square.'

'Oh, you don't want to go to Torrington Square?' He seemed amused and wary, but more wary than amused.

'It's such a lovely night, so warm. I don't want to go home just yet. I think I'll go and sit in Hyde Park.'

'Not Torrington Square,' he shouted through the window.

The taxi drew up.

'Damn his eyes, what's he done that for.'

The driver got down and opened the door.

'Here, where am I going to? This is the third time you've changed your mind since you 'ailed me.'

'You'll go where you're damn well told.'

'Well where am I damn well told?'

'Go to the Marble Arch.'

' 'Yde Park,' the driver said, looking us up and down and grinning broadly. Then he got back into his seat.

'I can't bear some of these chaps, can you?' the young man said.

When the taxi stopped at the end of Park Lane we both got out without a word. The driver looked us up and down again scornfully before he started away.

'What do you want to do in Hyde Park? Look at the trees?'

He took my suitcase and walked along by my side.

'Yes, I want to look at the trees and not go back to the place where I live. Never go back.'

'I've never lived in a place I like,' I thought, 'never.'

'That does sound desperate. Well, let's see if we can find a secluded spot.'

'That chair over there will do,' I said. It was away from people under a tree. Not that people mattered much, for now it was night and they are never so frightening then.

I shut my eyes so that I could hear and smell the trees better. I imagined I could smell water too. The Serpentine – I didn't know we had walked so far.

He said, 'I can't leave you so disconsolate on this lovely night – this night of love and night of stars.' He gave a loud hiccup, and then another. 'That always happens when I've eaten quails.'

'It happens to me when I'm tight.'

'Does it?' He pulled another chair forward and sat down by my side. 'I can't leave you now until I know where you're going with that large suitcase and that desperate expression.'

I told him that I had just come back after a stay in the country, and he told me that he did not live in London, that his name was Melville and that he was at a loose end that evening.

'Did somebody let you down?'

'Oh, that's not important – not half so important as the desperate expression. I noticed that as soon as I saw you.'

'That's not despair, it's hunger,' I said, dropping into the backchat. 'Don't you know hunger when you see it?'

'Well, let's go and have something to eat, then. But where?' He looked at me uncertainly. 'Where?'

'We could go to the Apple Tree. Of course, it's a bit early, but we might be able to get kippers or eggs and bacon or sausages and mash.'

'The Apple Tree? I've heard of it. Could we go there?' he said, still eyeing me.

'We could indeed. You could come as my guest. I'm a member. I was one of the first members,' I boasted.

I had touched the right spring – even the feeling of his hand on my arm had changed. *Always the same spring to touch before the sneering expression will go out of their eyes and the sneering sound out of their voices. Think about it – it's very important.*

'Lots of pretty girls at the Apple Tree, aren't there?' he said.

'I can't promise anything. It's a bad time of year for the Apple Tree, the singing and the gold.'

'Now what are you talking about?'

'Somebody I know calls it that.'

'But you'll be there.' He pulled his chair closer and looked round cautiously before he kissed me. 'And you're an awfully pretty girl, aren't you? . . . The Apple Tree, the singing and the gold. I like that.'

'Better than "Night of love and night of stars"?'

'Oh, they're not in the same street.'

I thought, 'How do you know what's in what street? How do they know who's fifth-rate, who's first-rate and where the devouring spider lives?'

'You don't really mind where we go, do you?' he said.

'I don't mind at all.'

He took his arm away. 'It was odd our meeting like that, wasn't it?'

'I don't think so. I don't think it was odd at all.'

After a silence, 'I haven't been very swift in the uptake, have I?' he said.

'No, you haven't. Now, let's be off to the Apple Tree, the singing and the gold.'

'Oh, damn the Apple Tree. I know a better place than that.'

'I've been persuaded to taste it before,' Marston said. 'It tasted exactly as I thought it would.'

And everything was exactly as I had expected. The knowing

waiters, the touch of the ice-cold wine glass, the red plush chairs, the food you don't notice, the gold-framed mirror, the bed in the room beyond that always looks as if its ostentatious whiteness hides dinginess. . . .

But Marston should have said, 'It tastes of nothing, my dear, it tastes of nothing. . . .'

When we got out into Leicester Square again I had forgotten Marston and only thought about how, when we had nothing better to do, Estelle and I would go to the Corner House or to some cheap restaurant in Soho and have dinner. She was so earnest when it came to food. 'You must have one good meal a day,' she would say, 'it is *necessary.*' Escalope de veau and fried potatoes and brussels sprouts, we usually had, and then crème caramel or compôte de fruits. And she seemed to be walking along by my side, wearing her blue suit and her white blouse, her high heels tapping. But as we turned the corner by the Hippodrome she vanished. I thought 'I shall never see her again – I know it.'

In the taxi he said, 'I don't forget addresses, do I?'

'No, you don't.'

To keep myself awake I began to sing 'Mr Brown, Mr Brown, Had a violin . . .'

'Are you on the stage?'

'I was. I started my brilliant and successful career like so many others, in the chorus. But I wasn't a success.'

'What a shame! Why?'

'Because I couldn't say "epigrammatic".'

He laughed – really laughed that time.

'The stage manager had the dotty idea of pulling me out of my obscurity and giving me a line to say. The line was "Oh, Lottie, Lottie, don't be epigrammatic". I rehearsed it and rehearsed it, but when it came to the night it was just a blank.'

At the top of Charing Cross Road the taxi was held up. We

were both laughing so much that people turned round and stared at us.

'It was one of the most dreadful moments of my life, and I shan't ever forget it. There was the stage manager, mouthing at me from the wings – he was the prompter too and he also played a small part, the family lawyer – and there he was all dressed up in grey-striped trousers and a black tail-coat and top hat and silver side-whiskers, and there I was, in a yellow dress and a large straw hat and a green sunshade and a lovely background of an English castle and garden – half ruined and half not, you know – and a chorus of footmen and maids, and my mind a complete blank.'

The taxi started again. 'Well, what happened?'

'Nothing. After one second the other actors went smoothly on. I remember the next line. It was "Going to Ascot? Well, if you don't get into the Royal Enclosure when you *are* there I'm no judge of character".'

'But what about the audience?'

'Oh, the audience weren't surprised because, you see, they had never expected me to speak at all. Well, here we are.'

I gave him my latchkey and he opened the door.

'A formidable key! It's like the key of a prison,' he said.

Everyone had gone to bed and there wasn't even a ghost of Estelle's scent in the hall.

'We must see each other again,' he said. 'Please. Couldn't you write to me at – ' He stopped. 'No, I'll write to you. If you're ever – I'll write to you anyway.'

I said, 'Do you know what I want? I want a gold bracelet with blue stones in it. Not too blue – the darker blue I prefer.'

'Oh, well.' He was wary again. 'I'll do my best, but I'm not one of these plutocrats, you know.'

'Don't you dare to come back without it. But I'm going away for a few weeks. I'll be here again in September.'

'All right, I'll see you in September, Petronella,' he said chirpily, anxious to be off. 'And you've been so sweet to me.'

'The pleasure was all mine.'

He shook his head. 'Now, Lottie, Lottie, don't be epigrammatic.'

I thought, 'I daresay he would be nice if one got to know him. I daresay, perhaps . . .' listening to him tapping good-bye on the other side of the door. I tapped back twice and then started up the stairs. Past the door of Estelle's room, not feeling a thing as I passed it, because she had gone and I knew she would not ever come back.

In my room I stood looking out of the window, remembering my yellow dress, the blurred mass of the audience and the face of one man in the front row seen quite clearly, and how I thought, as quick as lightning. 'Help me, tell me what I have forgotten.' But though he had looked, as it seemed, straight into my eyes, and though I was sure he knew exactly what I was thinking, he had not helped me. He had only smiled. He had left me in that moment that seemed like years standing there until through the dreadful blankness of my mind I had heard a high, shrill, cockney voice saying, 'Going to Ascot?' and seen the stage manager frown and shake his head at me.

'My God, I must have looked a fool,' I thought, laughing and feeling the tears running down my face.

'What a waste of good tears!' the other girls had told me when I cried in the dressing-room that night. And I heard myself saying out loud in an affected voice, 'Oh, the waste, the waste, the waste!'

But that did not last long.

'What's the time?' I thought, and because I wasn't sleepy any longer I sat down in the chair by the window, waiting for the clock outside to strike.

The Day they Burned the Books

My friend Eddie was a small, thin boy. You could see the blue veins in his wrists and temples. People said that he had consumption and wasn't long for this world. I loved, but sometimes despised him.

His father, Mr Sawyer, was a strange man. Nobody could make out what he was doing in our part of the world at all. He was not a planter or a doctor or a lawyer or a banker. He didn't keep a store. He wasn't a schoolmaster or a government official. He wasn't – that was the point – a gentleman. We had several resident romantics who had fallen in love with the moon on the Caribees – they were all gentlemen and quite unlike Mr Sawyer who hadn't an 'h' in his composition. Besides, he detested the moon and everything else about the Caribbean and he didn't mind telling you so.

He was agent for a small steamship line which in those days linked up Venezuela and Trinidad with the smaller islands, but he couldn't make much out of that. He must have a private income, people decided, but they never decided why he had chosen to settle in a place he didn't like and to marry a coloured woman. Though a decent, respectable, nicely educated coloured woman, mind you.

Mrs Sawyer must have been very pretty once but, what with one thing and another, that was in days gone by.

When Mr Sawyer was drunk – this often happened – he used to be very rude to her. She never answered him.

'Look at the nigger showing off,' he would say; and she would smile as if she knew she ought to see the joke but couldn't. 'You damned, long-eyed, gloomy half-caste, you don't smell right,' he would say; and she never answered, not even to whisper, 'You don't smell right to me, either.'

The story went that once they had ventured to give a dinner party and that when the servant, Mildred, was bringing in coffee, he had pulled Mrs Sawyer's hair. 'Not a wig, you see,' he bawled. Even then, if you can believe it, Mrs Sawyer had laughed and tried to pretend that it was all part of the joke, this mysterious, obscure, sacred English joke.

But Mildred told the other servants in the town that her eyes had gone wicked, like a soucriant's eyes, and that afterwards she had picked up some of the hair he pulled out and put it in an envelope, and that Mr Sawyer ought to look out (hair is obeah as well as hands).

Of course, Mrs Sawyer had her compensations. They lived in a very pleasant house in Hill Street. The garden was large and they had a fine mango tree, which bore prolifically. The fruit was small, round, very sweet and juicy – a lovely, red-and-yellow colour when it was ripe. Perhaps it was one of the compensations, I used to think.

Mr Sawyer built a room on to the back of this house. It was unpainted inside and the wood smelt very sweet. Bookshelves lined the walls. Every time the Royal Mail steamer came in it brought a package for him, and gradually the empty shelves filled.

Once I went there with Eddie to borrow *The Arabian Nights*. That was on a Saturday afternoon, one of those hot, still afternoons when you felt that everything had gone to sleep, even the water in the gutters. But Mrs Sawyer was not asleep. She put her head in at the door and looked at us, and I knew that she hated the room and hated the books.

It was Eddie with the pale blue eyes and straw-coloured hair – the living image of his father, though often as silent as his mother – who first infected me with doubts about 'home', meaning England. He would be so quiet when others who had never seen it – none of us had ever seen it – were talking about its delights, gesticulating freely as we talked – London, the beautiful, rosy-cheeked ladies, the theatres, the shops, the fog, the blazing coal fires in winter, the exotic food (whitebait eaten to the sound of violins), strawberries and cream – the word 'strawberries' always spoken with a guttural and throaty sound which we imagined to be the proper English pronunciation.

'I don't like strawberries,' Eddie said on one occasion.

'You *don't like* strawberries?'

'No, and I don't like daffodils either. Dad's always going on about them. He says they lick the flowers here into a cocked hat and I bet that's a lie.'

We were all too shocked to say, 'You don't know a thing about it.' We were so shocked that nobody spoke to him for the rest of the day. But I for one admired him. I also was tired of learning and reciting poems in praise of daffodils, and my relations with the few 'real' English boys and girls I had met were awkward. I had discovered that if I called myself English they would snub me haughtily: 'You're not English; you're a horrid colonial.' 'Well, I don't much want to be English,' I would say. 'It's much more fun to be French or Spanish or something like that – and, as a matter of fact, I am a bit.' Then I was too killingly funny, quite ridiculous. Not only a horrid colonial, but also ridiculous. Heads I win, tails you lose – that was the English. I had thought about all this, and thought hard, but I had never dared to tell anybody what I thought and I realized that Eddie had been very bold.

But he was bold, and stronger than you would think. For one thing, he never felt the heat; some coldness in his fair skin resisted it. He didn't burn red or brown, he didn't freckle much.

Hot days seemed to make him feel especially energetic. 'Now we'll run twice round the lawn and then you can pretend you're dying of thirst in the desert and that I'm an Arab chieftain bringing you water.'

'You must drink slowly,' he would say, 'for if you're very thirsty and you drink quickly you die.'

So I learnt the voluptuousness of drinking slowly when you are very thirsty – small mouthful by small mouthful, until the glass of pink, iced Coca-Cola was empty.

Just after my twelfth birthday Mr Sawyer died suddenly, and as Eddie's special friend I went to the funeral, wearing a new white dress. My straight hair was damped with sugar and water the night before and plaited into tight little plaits, so that it should be fluffy for the occasion.

When it was all over everybody said how nice Mrs Sawyer had looked, walking like a queen behind the coffin and crying her eyeballs out at the right moment, and wasn't Eddie a funny boy? He hadn't cried at all.

After this Eddie and I took possession of the room with the books. No one else ever entered it, except Mildred to sweep and dust in the mornings, and gradually the ghost of Mr Sawyer pulling Mrs Sawyer's hair faded, though this took a little time. The blinds were always half-way down and going in out of the sun was like stepping into a pool of brown-green water. It was empty except for the bookshelves, a desk with a green baize top and a wicker rocking-chair.

'My room,' Eddie called it. 'My books,' he would say, 'my books.'

I don't know how long this lasted. I don't know whether it was weeks after Mr Sawyer's death or months after, that I see myself and Eddie in the room. But there we are and there, unexpectedly, are Mrs Sawyer and Mildred. Mrs Sawyer's mouth tight, her eyes pleased. She is pulling all the books out of the shelves and piling them into two heaps. The big, fat glossy ones – the good-looking ones, Mildred explains in a whisper – lie in one heap. The *Encyclopaedia Britannica*, *British Flowers*, *Birds and Beasts*, various histories, books with maps, Froude's *English in the West Indies* and so on – they are going to be sold. The unimportant books, with paper covers or damaged covers or torn pages, lie in another heap. They are going to be burnt – yes, burnt.

Mildred's expression was extraordinary as she said that – half hugely delighted, half-shocked, even frightened. And as for Mrs Sawyer – well, I knew bad temper (I had often seen it), I knew rage, but this was hate. I recognized the difference at once and stared at her curiously. I edged closer to her so that I could see the titles of the books she was handling.

It was the poetry shelf. *Poems*, Lord Byron, *Poetical Works*, Milton, and so on. Vlung, vlung, vlung – all thrown into the heap that were to be sold. But a book by Christina Rossetti, though also bound in leather, went into the heap that was to be burnt, and by a flicker in Mrs Sawyer's eyes I knew that worse than men who wrote books were women who wrote books – infinitely worse. Men could be mercifully shot; women must be tortured.

Mrs Sawyer did not seem to notice that we were there, but she was breathing free and easy and her hands had got the rhythm of tearing and pitching. She looked beautiful, too – beautiful as the sky outside which was a very dark blue, or the mango tree, long sprays of brown and gold.

When Eddie said 'No', she did not even glance at him.

'No,' he said again in a high voice. 'Not that one. I was reading that one.'

She laughed and he rushed at her, his eyes starting out of his head, shrieking, 'Now I've got to hate you too. Now I hate you too.'

He snatched the book out of her hand and gave her a violent push. She fell into the rocking-chair.

Well, I wasn't going to be left out of all this, so I grabbed a book from the condemned pile and dived under Mildred's outstretched arm.

Then we were both in the garden. We ran along the path, bordered with crotons. We pelted down the path, though they did not follow us and we could hear Mildred laughing – kyah, kyah, kyah, kyah. As I ran I put the book I had taken into the loose front of my brown holland dress. It felt warm and alive.

When we got into the street we walked sedately, for we feared the black children's ridicule. I felt very happy, because I had saved this book and it was my book and I would read it from the beginning to the triumphant words 'The End'. But I was uneasy when I thought of Mrs Sawyer.

'What will she do?' I said.

'Nothing,' Eddie said. 'Not to me.'

He was white as a ghost in his sailor suit, a blue-white even in the setting sun, and his father's sneer was clamped on his face.

'But she'll tell your mother all sorts of lies about you,' he said. 'She's an awful liar. She can't make up a story to save her life, but she makes up lies about people all right.'

'My mother won't take any notice of her,' I said. Though I was not at all sure.

'Why not? Because she's . . . because she isn't white?'

Well, I knew the answer to that one. Whenever the subject was brought up – people's relations and whether they had a drop of coloured blood or whether they hadn't – my father would grow impatient and interrupt. 'Who's white?' he would say. 'Damned few.'

So *I* said, 'Who's white? Damned few.'

'You can go to the devil,' Eddie said. 'She's prettier than your mother. When she's asleep her mouth smiles and she has curling eyelashes and quantities and quantities and *quantities* of hair.'

'Yes,' I said truthfully. 'She's prettier than my mother.'

It was a red sunset that evening, a huge, sad, frightening sunset.

'Look, let's go back,' I said. 'If you're sure she won't be vexed with you, let's go back. It'll be dark soon.'

At his gate he asked me not to go. 'Don't go yet, don't go yet.'

We sat under the mango tree and I was holding his hand when he began to cry. Drops fell on my hand like the water from the dripstone in the filter in our yard. Then I began to cry too and when I felt my own tears on my hand I thought, 'Now perhaps we're married.'

'Yes, certainly, now we're married,' I thought. But I didn't say anything. I didn't say a thing until I was sure he had stopped. Then I asked, 'What's your book?'

'It's *Kim*,' he said. 'But it got torn. It starts at page twenty now. What's the one you took?'

'I don't know; it's too dark to see,' I said.

When I got home I rushed into my bedroom and locked the door because I knew that this book was the most important thing that had ever happened to me and I did not want anybody to be there when I looked at it.

But I was very disappointed, because it was in French and seemed dull. *Fort Comme La Mort*, it was called. . . .

Let them Call it Jazz

ONE bright Sunday morning in July I have trouble with my Notting Hill landlord because he ask for a month's rent in advance. He tell me this after I live there since winter, settling up every week without fail. I have no job at the time, and if I give the money he want there's not much left. So I refuse. The man drunk already at that early hour, and he abuse me – all talk, he can't frighten me. But his wife is a bad one – now she walk in my room and say she must have cash. When I tell her no, she give my suitcase one kick and it burst open. My best dress fall out, then she laugh and give another kick. She say month in advance is usual, and if I can't pay find somewhere else.

Don't talk to me about London. Plenty people there have heart like stone. Any complaint – the answer is 'prove it'. But if nobody see and bear witness for me, how to prove anything? So I pack up and leave, I think better not have dealings with that woman. She too cunning, and Satan don't lie worse.

I walk about till a place nearby is open where I can have coffee and a sandwich. There I start talking to a man at my table. He talk to me already, I know him, but I don't know his name. After a while he ask, 'What's the matter? Anything wrong?'

and when I tell him my trouble he say I can use an empty flat he own till I have time to look around.

This man is not at all like most English people. He see very quick, and he decide very quick. English people take long time to decide – you three-quarter dead before they make up their mind about you. Too besides, he speak very matter of fact, as if it's nothing. He speak as if he realize well what it is to live like I do – that's why I accept and go.

He tell me somebody occupy the flat till last week, so I find everything all right, and he tell me how to get there – three-quarters of an hour from Victoria Station, up a steep hill, turn left, and I can't mistake the house. He give me the keys and an envelope with a telephone number on the back. Underneath is written 'After 6 p.m. ask for Mr Sims'.

In the train that evening I think myself lucky, for to walk about London on a Sunday with nowhere to go – that take the heart out of you.

I find the place and the bedroom of the downstairs flat is nicely furnished – two looking glass, wardrobe, chest of drawers, sheets, everything. It smell of jasmine scent, but it smell strong of damp too.

I open the door opposite and there's a table, a couple chairs, a gas stove and a cupboard, but this room so big it look empty. When I pull the blind up I notice the paper peeling off and mushrooms growing on the walls – you never see such a thing.

The bathroom the same, all the taps rusty. I leave the two other rooms and make up the bed. Then I listen, but I can't hear one sound. Nobody come in, nobody go out of that house. I lie awake for a long time, then I decide not to stay and in the morning I start to get ready quickly before I change my mind. I want to wear my best dress, but it's a funny thing – when I take up that dress and remember how my landlady kick it I cry.

I cry and I can't stop. When I stop I feel tired to my bones, tired like old woman. I don't want to move again – I have to force myself. But in the end I get out in the passage and there's a postcard for me. 'Stay as long as you like. I'll be seeing you soon – Friday probably. Not to worry.' It isn't signed, but I don't feel so sad and I think, 'All right, I wait here till he come. Perhaps he know of a job for me.'

Nobody else live in the house but a couple on the top floor – quiet people and they don't trouble me. I have no word to say against them.

First time I meet the lady she's opening the front door and she give me a very inquisitive look. But next time she smile a bit and I smile back – once she talk to me. She tell me the house very old, hundred and fifty year old, and she and her husband live there since long time. 'Valuable property,' she says, 'it could have been saved, but nothing done of course.' Then she tells me that as to the present owner – if he is the owner – well he have to deal with local authorities and she believe they make difficulties. 'These people are determined to pull down all the lovely old houses – it's shameful.'

So I agree that many things shameful. But what to do ? What to do ? I say it have an elegant shape, it make the other houses in the street look cheap trash, and she seem pleased. That's true too. The house sad and out of place, especially at night. But it have style. The second floor shut up, and as for my flat, I go in the two empty rooms once, but never again.

Underneath was the cellar, full of old boards and broken-up furniture – I see a big rat there one day. It was no place to be alone in I tell you, and I get the habit of buying a bottle of wine most evenings, for I don't like whisky and the rum here no good. It don't even *taste* like rum. You wonder what they do to it.

After I drink a glass or two I can sing and when I sing all the misery goes from my heart. Sometimes I make up songs but next morning I forget them, so other times I sing the old ones like *Tantalizin'* or *Don't Trouble Me Now*.

I think I go but I don't go. Instead I wait for the evening and the wine and that's all. Everywhere else I live – well, it doesn't matter to me, but this house is different – empty and no noise and full of shadows, so that sometimes you ask yourself what make all those shadows in an empty room.

I eat in the kitchen, then I clean up everything nice and have a bath for coolness. Afterwards I lean my elbows on the windowsill and look at the garden. Red and blue flowers mix up with the weeds and there are five–six apple trees. But the fruit drop and lie in the grass, so sour nobody want it. At the back, near the wall, is a bigger tree – this garden certainly take up a lot of room, perhaps that's why they want to pull the place down.

Not much rain all the summer, but not much sunshine either. More of a glare. The grass get brown and dry, the weeds grow tall, the leaves on the trees hang down. Only the red flowers – the poppies – stand up to that light, everything else look weary.

I don't trouble about money, but what with wine and shillings for the slot-meters, it go quickly; so I don't waste much on food. In the evening I walk outside – not by the apple trees but near the street – it's not so lonely.

There's no wall here and I can see the woman next door looking at me over the hedge. At first I say good evening, but she turn away her head, so afterwards I don't speak. A man is often with her, he wear a straw hat with a black ribbon and goldrim spectacles. His suit hang on him like it's too big. He's the husband it seems and he stare at me worse than his wife – he stare as if I'm wild animal let loose. Once I laugh in his face because why these people have to be like that? I don't bother them. In the end I get that I don't even give them one single glance. I have plenty other things to worry about.

To show you how I felt. I don't remember exactly. But I believe it's the second Saturday after I come that when I'm at the window just before I go for my wine I feel somebody's hand on my shoulder and it's Mr Sims. He must walk very quiet because I don't know a thing till he touch me.

He says hullo, then he tells me I've got terrible thin, do I ever eat. I say of course I eat but he goes on that it doesn't suit me at all to be so thin and he'll buy some food in the village. (That's the way he talk. There's no village here. You don't get away from London so quick.)

It don't seem to me he look very well himself, but I just say bring a drink instead, as I am not hungry.

He come back with three bottles – vermouth, gin and red wine. Then he ask if the little devil who was here last smash all the glasses and I tell him she smash some, I find the pieces. But not all. 'You fight with her, eh?'

He laugh, and he don't answer. He pour out the drinks then he says, 'Now, you eat up those sandwiches.'

Some men when they are there you don't worry so much. These sort of men you do all they tell you blindfold because they can take the trouble from your heart and make you think you're safe. It's nothing they say or do. It's a feeling they can give you. So I don't talk with him seriously – I don't want to spoil that evening. But I ask about the house and why it's so empty and he says:

'Has the old trout upstairs been gossiping?'

I tell him, 'She suppose they make difficulties for you.'

'It was a damn bad buy,' he says and talks about selling the lease or something. I don't listen much.

We were standing by the window then and the sun low. No more glare. He puts his hand over my eyes. 'Too big –

much too big for your face,' he says and kisses me like you kiss a baby. When he takes his hand away I see he's looking out at the garden and he says this – 'It gets you. My God it does.'

I know very well it's not me he means, so I ask him, 'Why sell it then? If you like it, keep it.'

'Sell what?' he says. 'I'm not talking about this damned house.'

I ask what he's talking about. 'Money,' he says. 'Money. That's what I'm talking about. Ways of making it.'

'I don't think so much of money. It don't like me and what do I care?' I was joking, but he turns around, his face quite pale and he tells me I'm a fool. He tells me I'll get push around all my life and die like a dog, only worse because they'd finish off a dog, but they'll let me live till I'm a caricature of myself. That's what he say, 'Caricature of yourself.' He say I'll curse the day I was born and everything and everybody in this bloody world before I'm done.

I tell him, 'No I'll never feel like that,' and he smiles, if you can call it a smile, and says he's glad I'm content with my lot. 'I'm disappointed in you, Selina. I thought you had more spirit.'

'If I contented that's all right,' I answer him, 'I don't see very many looking contented over here.' We're standing staring at each other when the door bell rings. 'That's a friend of mine,' he says. 'I'll let him in.'

As to the friend, he's all dressed up in stripe pants and a black jacket and he's carrying a brief-case. Very ordinary looking but with a soft kind of voice.

'Maurice, this is Selina Davis,' says Mr Sims, and Maurice smiles very kind but it don't mean much, then he looks at his watch and says they ought to be getting along.

At the door Mr Sims tells me he'll see me next week and I answer straight out, 'I won't be here next week because I want a job and I won't get one in this place.'

'Just what I'm going to talk about. Give it a week longer, Selina.'

I say, 'Perhaps I stay a few more days. Then I go. Perhaps I go before.'

'Oh no you won't go,' he says.

They walk to the gates quickly and drive off in a yellow car. Then I feel eyes on me and it's the woman and her husband in the next door garden watching. The man make some remark and she look at me so hateful, so hating I shut the front door quick.

I don't want more wine. I want to go to bed early because I must think. I must think about money. It's true I don't care for it. Even when somebody steal my savings – this happen soon after I get to the Notting Hill house – I forget it soon. About thirty pounds they steal. I keep it roll up in a pair of stockings, but I go to the drawer one day, and no money. In the end I have to tell the police. They ask me exact sum and I say I don't count it lately, about thirty pounds. 'You don't know how much?' they say. 'When did you count it last? Do you remember? Was it before you move or after?'

I get confuse, and I keep saying, 'I don't remember,' though I remember well I see it two days before. They don't believe me and when a policeman come to the house I hear the landlady tell him, 'She certainly had no money when she came here. She wasn't able to pay a month's rent in advance for her room though it's a rule in this house.' 'These people terrible liars,' she say and I think 'it's you a terrible liar, because when I come you tell me weekly or monthly as you like.' It's from that time she don't speak to me and perhaps it's she take it. All I know is I never see one penny of my savings again, all I know is they pretend I never have any, but as it's gone, no use to cry about it. Then my mind goes to my father, for my father is a white man and I think a lot about him. If I could see him only once, for I too small to remember when he was there. My mother is fair coloured woman, fairer than I am they say, and she don't stay long with me either. She have a chance to go to Venezuela when I three-four year old and she never come back. She send money instead. It's my grandmother take care of me. She's quite dark and what we call 'country-cookie' but she's the best I know.

She save up all the money my mother send, she don't keep one penny for herself – that's how I get to England. I was a bit late in going to school regular, getting on for twelve years, but I can sew very beautiful, excellent – so I think I get a good job – in London perhaps.

However here they tell me all this fine handsewing take too long. Waste of time – too slow. They want somebody to work quick and to hell with the small stitches. Altogether it don't look so good for me, I must say, and I wish I could see my father. I have his name – Davis. But my grandmother tell me, 'Every word that come out of that man's mouth a damn lie. He is certainly first class liar, though no class otherwise.' So perhaps I have not even his real name.

Last thing I see before I put the light out is the postcard on the dressing table. 'Not to worry.'

Not to worry! Next day is Sunday, and it's on the Monday the people next door complain about me to the police. That evening the woman is by the hedge, and when I pass her she says in very sweet quiet voice, '*Must* you stay? *Can't* you go?' I don't answer. I walk out in the street to get rid of her. But she run inside her house to the window, she can still see me. Then I start to sing, so she can understand I'm not afraid of her. The husband call out: 'If you don't stop that noise I'll send for the police.' I answer them quite short. I say, 'You go to hell and take your wife with you.' And I sing louder.

The police come pretty quick – two of them. Maybe they

just round the corner. All I can say about police, and how they behave is I think it all depend who they dealing with. Of my own free will I don't want to mix up with police. No.

One man says, you can't cause this disturbance here. But the other asks a lot of questions. What is my name? Am I tenant of a flat in No. 17? How long have I lived there? Last address and so on. I get vexed the way he speak and I tell him, 'I come here because somebody steal my savings. Why you don't look for my money instead of bawling at me? I work hard for my money. All-you don't do one single thing to find it.'

'What's she talking about?' the first one says, and the other one tells me, 'You can't make that noise here. Get along home. You've been drinking.'

I see that woman looking at me and smiling, and other people at their windows, and I'm so angry I bawl at them too. I say, 'I have absolute and perfect right to be in the street same as anybody else, and I have absolute and perfect right to ask the police why they don't even look for my money when it disappear. It's because a dam' English thief take it you don't look,' I say. The end of all this is that I have to go before a magistrate, and he fine me five pounds for drunk and disorderly, and he give me two weeks to pay.

When I get back from the court I walk up and down the kitchen, up and down, waiting for six o'clock because I have no five pounds left, and I don't know what to do. I telephone at six and a woman answers me very short and sharp, then Mr Sims comes along and he don't sound too pleased either when I tell him what happen. 'Oh Lord!' he says, and I say I'm sorry. 'Well don't panic,' he says, 'I'll pay the fine. But look, I don't think. . . .' Then he breaks off and talk to some other person in the room. He goes on, 'Perhaps better not stay at No. 17. I think I can arrange something else. I'll call for you Wednesday – Saturday latest. Now behave till then.' And he hang up before I can answer that I don't want to wait till Wednesday, much less Saturday. I want to get out of that house double quick and with no delay. First I think I ring back, then I think better not as he sound so vex.

I get ready, but Wednesday he don't come, and Saturday he don't come. All the week I stay in the flat. Only once I go out and arrange for bread, milk and eggs to be left at the door, and seems to me I meet up with a lot of policemen. They don't look at me, but they see me all right. I don't want to drink – I'm all the time listening, listening and thinking, how can I leave before I know if my fine is paid? I tell myself the police let me know, that's certain. But I don't trust them. What they care? The answer is Nothing. Nobody care. One afternoon I knock at the old lady's flat upstairs, because I get the idea she give me good advice. I can hear her moving about and talking, but she don't answer and I never try again.

Nearly two weeks pass like that, then I telephone. It's the woman speaking and she say, 'Mr Sims is not in London at present.' I ask, 'When will he be back – it's urgent,' and she hang up. I'm not surprised. Not at all. I knew that would happen. All the same I feel heavy like lead. Near the phone box is a chemist's shop, so I ask him for something to make me sleep, the day is bad enough, but to lie awake all night – Ah no! He gives me a little bottle marked '*One or two tablets only*' and I take three when I go to bed because more and more I think that sleeping is better than no matter what else. However, I lie there, eyes wide open as usual, so I take three more. Next thing I know the room is full of sunlight, so it must be late afternoon, but the lamp is still on. My head turn around and I can't think well at all. At first I ask myself how I get to the place. Then it comes to me, but in pictures – like the landlady kicking my dress, and when I take my ticket at Victoria Station, and Mr Sims telling me to eat the sandwiches, but I can't remember everything clear, and I feel very giddy and sick. I take in the milk and eggs at the door, go in the kitchen, and try to eat but the food hard to swallow.

It's when I'm putting the things away that I see the bottles – pushed back on the lowest shelf in the cupboard.

There's a lot of drink left, and I'm glad I tell you. Because I can't bear the way I feel. Not any more. I mix a gin and vermouth and I drink it quick, then I mix another and drink it slow by the window. The garden looks different, like I never see it before. I know quite well what I must do, but it's late now – tomorrow. I have one more drink, of wine this time, and then a song come in my head, I sing it and I dance it, and more I sing, more I am sure this is the best tune that has ever come to me in all my life.

The sunset light from the window is gold colour. My shoes sound loud on the boards. So I take them off, my stockings too and go on dancing but the room feel shut in, I can't breathe, and I go outside still singing. Maybe I dance a bit too. I forget all about that woman till I hear her saying, 'Henry, look at this.' I turn around and I see her at the window. 'Oh yes, I wanted to speak with you,' I say, 'Why bring the police and get me in bad trouble? Tell me that.'

'And you tell *me* what you're doing here at all,' she says. 'This is a respectable neighbourhood.'

Then the man come along. 'Now young woman, take yourself off. You ought to be ashamed of this behaviour.'

'It's disgraceful,' he says, talking to his wife, but loud so I can hear, and she speaks loud too – for once. 'At least the other tarts that crook installed here were *white* girls,' she says.

'You a dam' fouti liar,' I say. 'Plenty of those girls in your country already. Numberless as the sands on the shore. You don't need me for that.'

'You're not a howling success at it certainly.' Her voice

sweet sugar again. 'And you won't be seeing much more of your friend Mr Sims. He's in trouble too. Try somewhere else. Find somebody else. If you can, of course.' When she say that my arm moves of itself. I pick up a stone and bam! through the window. Not the one they are standing at but the next, which is of coloured glass, green and purple and yellow.

I never see a woman look so surprise. Her mouth fall open she so full of surprise. I start to laugh, louder and louder – I laugh like my grandmother, with my hands on my hips and my head back. (When she laugh like that you can hear her to the end of our street.) At last I say, 'Well, I'm sorry. An accident. I get it fixed tomorrow early.' 'That glass is irreplaceable,' the man says. 'Irreplaceable.' 'Good thing,' I say, 'those colours look like they sea-sick to me. I buy you a better windowglass.'

He shake his fist at me. 'You won't be let off with a fine this time,' he says. Then they draw the curtains. I call out at them. 'You run away. Always you run away. Ever since I come here you hunt me down because I don't answer back. It's you shameless.' I try to sing 'Don't trouble me now'.

Don't trouble me now
You without honour.
Don't walk in my footstep
You without shame.

But my voice don't sound right, so I get back indoors and drink one more glass of wine – still wanting to laugh, and still thinking of my grandmother for that is one of her songs.

It's about a man whose doudou give him the go-by when she find somebody rich and he sail away to Panama. Plenty people die there of fever when they make that Panama canal so long ago. But he don't die. He come back with dollars and the girl meet him on the jetty, all dressed up and smiling. Then he sing to her, 'You without honour, you without shame.' It sound good in Martinique patois too: 'Sans honte'.

Afterwards I ask myself, 'Why I do that? It's not like me. But if they treat you wrong over and over again the hour strike when you burst out that's what.'

Too besides, Mr Sims can't tell me now I have no spirit. I don't care, I sleep quickly and I'm glad I break the woman's ugly window. But as to my own song it go *right* away and it never come back. A pity.

Next morning the doorbell ringing wake me up. The people upstairs don't come down, and the bell keeps on like fury self. So I go to look, and there is a policeman and a policewoman outside. As soon as I open the door the woman put her foot in it. She wear sandals and thick stockings and I never see a foot so big or so bad. It look like it want to mash up the whole world. Then she come in after the foot, and her face not so pretty either. The policeman tell me my fine is not paid and people make serious complaints about me, so they're taking me back to the magistrate. He show me a paper and I look at it, but I don't read it. The woman push me in the bedroom, and tell me to get dress quickly, but I just stare at her, because I think perhaps I wake up soon. Then I ask her what I must wear. She say she suppose I had some clothes on yesterday. Or not? 'What's it matter, wear anything,' she says. But I find clean underclothes and stockings and my shoes with high heels and I comb my hair. I start to file my nails, because I think they too long for magistrate's court but she get angry. 'Are you coming quietly or aren't you?' she says. So I go with them and we get in a car outside.

I wait for a long time in a room full of policemen. They come in, they go out, they telephone, they talk in low voices. Then it's my turn, and first thing I notice in the court room is a man with frowning black eyebrows. He sit below the magistrate, he dressed in black and he so handsome I can't take my eyes off him. When he see that he frown worse than before.

First comes a policeman to testify I cause disturbance, and then comes the old gentleman from next door. He repeat that bit about nothing but the truth so help me God. Then he says I make dreadful noise at night and use abominable language, and dance in obscene fashion. He says when they try to shut the curtains because his wife so terrify of me, I throw stones and break a valuable stain-glass window. He say his wife get serious injury if she'd been hit, and as it is she in terrible nervous condition and the doctor is with her. I think, 'Believe me, if I aim at your wife I hit your wife – that's certain.' 'There was no provocation,' he says. 'None at all.' Then another lady from across the street says this is true. She heard no provocation whatsoever, and she swear that they shut the curtains but I go on insulting them and using filthy language and she saw all this and heard it.

The magistrate is a little gentleman with a quiet voice, but I'm very suspicious of these quiet voices now. He ask me why I don't pay my fine, and I say because I haven't the money. I get the idea they want to find out all about Mr Sims – they listen so very attentive. But they'll find out nothing from me. He ask how long I have the flat and I say I don't remember. I know they want to trip me up like they trip me up about my savings so I won't answer. At last he ask if I have anything to say as I can't be allowed to go on being a nuisance. I think, 'I'm nuisance to you because I have no money that's all.' I want to speak up and tell him how they steal all my savings, so when my landlord asks for month's rent I haven't got it to give. I want to tell him the woman next door provoke me since long time and call me bad names but she have a soft sugar voice and nobody hear – that's why I broke her window, but I'm ready to buy another after all. I want to say all I do is sing in that old garden, and I want to say this in decent quiet voice. But I hear myself talking loud and I see my hands wave in the air. Too besides it's no use, they won't believe me, so I don't finish. I stop, and I feel the tears on my face. 'Prove it.' That's all they will say. They whisper, they whisper. They nod, they nod.

Next thing I'm in a car again with a different policewoman, dressed very smart. Not in uniform. I ask her where she's taking me and she says 'Holloway' just that 'Holloway'.

I catch hold of her hand because I'm afraid. But she takes it away. Cold and smooth her hand slide away and her face is china face – smooth like a doll and I think, 'This is the last time I ask anything from anybody. So help me God.'

The car come up to a black castle and little mean streets are all round it. A lorry was blocking up the castle gates. When it get by we pass through and I am in jail. First I stand in a line with others who are waiting to give up handbags and all belongings to a woman behind bars like in a post office. The girl in front bring out a nice compact, look like gold to me, lipstick to match and a wallet full of notes. The woman keep the money, but she give back the powder and lipstick and she half-smile. I have two pounds seven shillings and sixpence in pennies. She take my purse, then she throw me my compact (which is cheap), my comb and my handkerchief like everything in my bag is dirty. So I think, 'Here too, here too.' But I tell myself, 'Girl, what you expect, eh? They all like that. All.'

Some of what happen afterwards I forget, or perhaps better not remember. Seems to me they start by trying to frighten you. But they don't succeed with me for I don't care for nothing now, it's as if my heart hard like a rock and I can't feel.

Then I'm standing at the top of a staircase with a lot of women and girls. As we are going down I notice the railing very low on one side, very easy to jump, and a long way below there's the grey stone passage like it's waiting for you.

As I'm thinking this a uniform woman step up alongside quick and grab my arm. She say, 'Oh no you don't.'

I was just noticing the railing very low that's all – but what's the use of saying so.

Another long line waits for the doctor. It move forward slowly and my legs terrible tired. The girl in front is very young and she cry and cry. 'I'm scared,' she keeps saying. She's lucky in a way – as for me I never will cry again. It all dry up and hard in me now. That, and a lot besides. In the end I tell her to stop, because she doing just what these people want her to do.

She stop crying and start a long story, but while she is speaking her voice get very far away, and I find I can't see her face clear at all.

Then I'm in a chair, and one of those uniform women is pushing my head down between my knees, but let her push – everything go away from me just the same.

They put me in the hospital because the doctor say I'm sick. I have cell by myself and it's all right except I don't sleep. The things they say you mind I don't mind.

When they clang the door on me I think, 'You shut me in, but you shut all those other dam' devils *out*. They can't reach me now.'

At first it bothers me when they keep on looking at me all through the night. They open a little window in the doorway to do this. But I get used to it and get used to the night chemise they give me. It very thick, and to my mind it not very clean either – but what's that matter to me? Only the food I can't swallow – especially the porridge. The woman ask me sarcastic, 'Hunger striking?' But afterwards I can leave most of it, and she don't say nothing.

One day a nice girl comes around with books and she give me two, but I don't want to read so much. Beside one is about a murder, and the other is about a ghost and I don't think it's at all like those books tell you.

There is nothing I want now. It's no use. If they leave me in peace and quiet that's all I ask. The window is barred but not small, so I can see a little thin tree through the bars, and I like watching it.

After a week they tell me I'm better and I can go out with the others for exercise. We walk round and round one of the yards in that castle – it is fine weather and the sky is a kind of pale blue, but the yard is a terrible sad place. The sunlight fall down and die there. I get tired walking in high heels and I'm glad when that's over.

We can talk, and one day an old woman come up and ask me for dog-ends. I don't understand, and she start muttering at me like she very vexed. Another woman tell me she mean cigarette ends, so I say I don't smoke. But the old woman still look angry, and when we're going in she give me one push and I nearly fall down. I'm glad to get away from these people, and hear the door clang and take my shoes off.

Sometimes I think, 'I'm here because I wanted to sing' and I have to laugh. But there's a small looking glass in my cell and I see myself and I'm like somebody else. Like some strange new person. Mr Sims tell me I too thin, but what he say now to this person in the looking glass? So I don't laugh again.

Usually I don't think at all. Everything and everybody seem small and far away, that is the only trouble.

Twice the doctor come to see me. He don't say much and I don't say anything, because a uniform woman is always there. She look like she thinking, 'Now the lies start.' So I prefer not to speak. Then I'm sure they can't trip me up. Perhaps I there still, or in a worse place. But one day this happen.

We were walking round and round in the yard and I hear a woman singing – the voice come from high up, from one of the small barred windows. At first I don't believe it. Why should anybody sing here? Nobody want to sing in jail, nobody want to do anything. There's no reason, and you have no hope. I think I must be asleep, dreaming, but I'm awake all right and I see all the others are listening too. A nurse is with us that afternoon, not a policewoman. She stop and look up at the window.

It's a smoky kind of voice, and a bit rough sometimes, as if those old dark walls theyselves are complaining, because they see too much misery – too much. But it don't fall down and die in the courtyard; seems to me it could jump the gates of the jail easy and travel far, and nobody could stop it. I don't hear the words – only the music. She sing one verse and she begin another, then she break off sudden. Everybody starts walking again, and nobody says one word. But as we go in I ask the woman in front who was singing. 'That's the Holloway song,' she says. 'Don't you know it yet? She was singing from the punishment cells, and she tell the girls cheerio and never say die.' Then I have to go one way to the hospital block and she goes another so we don't speak again.

When I'm back in my cell I can't just wait for bed. I walk up and down and I think. 'One day I hear that song on trumpets and these walls will fall and rest.' I want to get out so bad I could hammer on the door, for I know now that anything can happen, and I don't want to stay lock up here and miss it.

Then I'm hungry. I eat everything they bring and in the morning I'm still so hungry I eat the porridge. Next time the doctor come he tells me I seem much better. Then I say a little of what really happen in that house. Not much. Very careful.

He look at me hard and kind of surprised. At the door he shake his finger and says, 'Now don't let me see you here again.'

That evening the woman tells me I'm going, but she's so upset about it I don't ask questions. Very early, before it's light she bangs the door open and shouts at me to hurry up. As we're going along the passages I see the girl who gave me the books. She's in a row with others doing exercises. Up Down, Up Down, Up. We pass quite close and I notice she's looking very pale and tired. It's crazy, it's all crazy. This up down business and everything else too. When they give me my money I remember I leave my compact in the cell, so I ask if I can go back for it. You should see that policewoman's face as she shoo me on.

There's no car, there's a van and you can't see through the windows. The third time it stop I get out with one other, a young girl, and it's the same magistrate's court as before.

The two of us wait in a small room, nobody else there, and after a while the girl say, 'What the hell are they doing? I don't want to spend all day here.' She go to the bell and she keep her finger press on it. When I look at her she say, 'Well, what are they *for*?' That girl's face is hard like a board – she could change faces with many and you wouldn't know the difference. But she get results certainly. A policeman come in, all smiling, and we go in the court. The same magistrate, the same frowning man sits below, and when I hear my fine is paid I want to ask who paid it, but he yells at me. 'Silence.'

I think I will never understand the half of what happen, but they tell me I can go, and I understand that. The magistrate ask if I'm leaving the neighbourhood and I say yes, then I'm out in the streets again, and it's the same fine weather, same feeling I'm dreaming.

When I get to the house I see two men talking in the garden. The front door and the door of the flat are both open. I go in, and the bedroom is empty, nothing but the glare streaming inside because they take the Venetian blinds away. As I'm wondering where my suitcase is, and the clothes I leave in the wardrobe, there's a knock and it's the old lady from upstairs carrying my case packed, and my coat is over her arm. She says she sees me come in. 'I kept your things for you.' I start to thank her but she turn her back and walk away. They like that here, and better not expect too much. Too besides, I bet they tell her I'm terrible person.

I go in the kitchen, but when I see they are cutting down the big tree at the back I don't stay to watch.

At the station I'm waiting for the train and a woman asks if I feel well. 'You look so tired,' she says. 'Have you come a long way?' I want to answer, 'I come so far I lose myself on that journey.' But I tell her, 'Yes, I am quite well. But I can't stand the heat.' She says she can't stand it either, and we talk about the weather till the train come in.

I'm not frightened of them any more – after all what else can they do? I know what to say and everything go like a clock works.

I get a room near Victoria where the landlady accept one pound in advance, and next day I find a job in the kitchen of a private hotel close by. But I don't stay there long. I hear of another job going in a big store – altering ladies' dresses and I get that. I lie and tell them I work in very expensive New York shop. I speak bold and smooth faced, and they never check up on me. I make a friend there – Clarice – very light coloured, very smart, she have a lot to do with the customers and she laugh at some of them behind their backs. But I say it's not their fault if the dress don't fit. Special dress for one person only – that's very expensive in London. So it's take in, or let out all the time. Clarice have two rooms not far from the store. She furnish them herself gradual and she gives parties sometimes Saturday nights. It's there I start whistling the Holloway song. A man comes up to me and says, 'Let's hear that again.' So I whistle it again (I never sing now) and he tells me 'Not bad'. Clarice have an old piano somebody give her to store and he plays the tune, jazzing it up. I say, 'No, not like that,' but everybody else say the way he do it is first class. Well I think no more of this till I get a letter from him telling me he has sold the song and as I was quite a help he encloses five pounds with thanks.

I read the letter and I could cry. For after all, that song was all I had. I don't belong nowhere really, and I haven't money to buy my way to belonging. I don't want to either.

But when that girl sing, she sing to me, and she sing for me. I was there because I was *meant* to be there. It was *meant* I should hear it – this I *know*.

Now I've let them play it wrong, and it will go from me like all the other songs – like everything. Nothing left for me at all.

But then I tell myself all this is foolishness. Even if they played it on trumpets, even if they played it just right, like I wanted – no walls would fall so soon. 'So let them call it jazz,' I think, and let them play it wrong. That won't make no difference to the song I heard.

I buy myself a dusty pink dress with the money.

Tigers Are Better-Looking

'MEIN Lieb, Mon Cher, My Dear, Amigo,' the letter began:

I'm off. I've been wanting to go for some time, as I'm sure you know, but was waiting for the moment when I had the courage to step out into the cold world again. Didn't feel like a farewell scene.

Apart from much that it is *better* not to go into, you haven't any idea how sick I am of all the phoney talk about Communism – and the phoney talk of the other lot too, if it comes to that. You people are exactly alike, whatever you call yourselves – Untouchable. Indispensable is the motto, and you'd pine to death if you hadn't someone to look down on and insult. I got the feeling that I was surrounded by a pack of timid tigers waiting to spring the moment anybody is in trouble or hasn't any money. *But tigers are better-looking, aren't they?*

I'm taking the coach to Plymouth. I have my plans.

I came to London with high hopes, but all I got out of it was a broken leg and enough sneers to last me for the next thirty years if I live so long, which may God forbid.

Don't think I'll forget how kind you were after my accident – having me to stay with you and all that. But assez means enough.

I've drunk the milk in the refrigerator. I was thirsty after that party last night, though if you call that a party I call it a wake. Besides, I know how you dislike the stuff (Freud! Bow-wow-wow!!) So you'll have to have your tea straight, my dear.

Good-bye. I'll write you again when times are better.

HANS

There was a postscript:

Mind you write a swell article today, you tame grey mare.

Mr Severn sighed. He had always known Hans would hop it sooner or later, so why this taste in his mouth, as if he had eaten dust?

A swell article.

The band in the Embankment Gardens played. It's the same old song once again. It's the same old tender refrain. *As the carriages came into sight some of the crowd cheered and a fat man said he couldn't see and he was going to climb a lamp-post. The figures in the carriages bowed from right to left – victims bowed to victimized. The bloodless sacrifice was being exhibited, the reminder that somewhere the sun is shining, even if it doesn't shine on everybody.*

' 'E looked just like a waxwork, didn't 'e?' a woman said with satisfaction. . . .

No, that would never do.

He looked out of the window at the Lunch Edition placards outside the newspaper shop opposite. 'JUBILEE PICTURES – PICTURES – PICTURES' and 'HEAT WAVE COMING'.

The flat over the shop was occupied by a raffish middle-aged woman. But today her lace-curtained windows, usually not unfriendly, added to his feeling of desolation. So did the words 'PICTURES – PICTURES – PICTURES'.

By six o'clock the floor was covered with newspapers and crumpled, discarded starts of the article which he wrote every week for an Australian paper.

He couldn't get the swing of it. The swing's the thing, as everybody knows – otherwise the cadence of the sentence. Once into it, and he could go ahead like an old horse trotting, saying anything that anybody liked.

'The tame grey mare,' he thought. Then he took up one of the newspapers and, because he had the statistical mania, began to count the advertisements. Two remedies for constipation, three for wind and stomach pains, three face creams, one skin food, one cruise to Morocco. At the end of the personal column, in small print, 'I will slay in the day of My wrath and spare not, saith the Lord God.' Who pays to put these things in anyway, who pays?

'This perpetual covert threat,' he thought. 'Everything's based on it. Disgusting. What Will They Say? And down at the bottom of the page you see what will happen to you if you don't toe the line. You will be slain and not spared. Threats and mockery, mockery and threats. . . .' And desolation, desertion and crumpled newspapers in the room.

The only comfort allowed was the money which would buy the warm glow of drink before eating, the Jubilee laughter afterwards. Jubilant – Jubilee – Joy. . . . Words whirled round in his head, but he could not make them take shape.

'If you won't, you bloody well won't,' he said to his typewriter before he rushed down the stairs, counting the steps as he went.

After two double whiskies at his usual pub, Time, which had dragged so drearily all day, began to move faster, began to gallop.

At half-past eleven Mr Severn was walking up and down Wardour Street between two young women. The things one does on the rebound.

He knew one of them fairly well – the fatter one. She was often at the pub and he liked talking to her, and sometimes stood her drinks because she was good-natured and never made him feel nervous. That was her secret. If fair was fair, it would be her epitaph: 'I have never made anybody feel nervous – on purpose.' Doomed, of course, for that very reason. But pleasant to talk to and, usually, to look at. Her name was Maidie – Maidie Richards.

He had never seen the other girl before. She was very young and fresh, with a really glittering smile and an accent he didn't quite recognize. She was called Heather Something-or-other. In the noisy pub he thought she said Hedda. 'What an unusual name!' he had remarked. 'I said Heather, not Hedda. Hedda! I wouldn't be seen dead with a name like that.' She was sharp, bright, self-confident – nothing flabby there. It was she who had suggested this final drink.

The girls argued. They each had an arm in one of Mr Severn's, and they argued across him. They got to Shaftesbury Avenue, turned and walked back.

'I tell you the place is in this street,' Heather said. 'The "Jim-Jam" – haven't you ever heard of it?'

'Are you sure?' Mr Severn asked.

'Of course I'm sure. It's on the left-hand side. We've missed it somehow.'

'Well, I'm sick of walking up and down looking for it,' Maidie said. 'It's a lousy hole anyway. I don't particularly want to go, do you?'

'Not particularly,' said Mr Severn.

'There it is,' Heather said. 'We've passed it twice. It's changed its name, that's what.'

They went up a narrow stone staircase and on the first landing a man with a yellow face appeared from behind drawn curtains and glared at them. Heather smiled. 'Good evening, Mr Johnson. I've brought two friends along.'

'Three of you? That'll be fifteen shillings.'

'I thought it was half a crown entrance,' Maidie said so aggressively that Mr Johnson looked at her with surprise and explained, 'This is a special night.'

'The orchestra's playing rotten, anyway,' Maidie remarked when they got into the room.

An elderly woman wearing steel-rimmed glasses was serving behind the bar. The mulatto who was playing the saxophone leaned forward and whooped.

'They play so rotten,' Maidie said, when the party was seated at a table against the wall, 'that you'd think they were doing it on purpose.'

'Oh stop grumbling,' Heather said. 'Other people don't agree with you. The place is packed every night. Besides, why should they play well. What's the difference?'

'Ah-ha,' Mr Severn said.

'There isn't any difference if you ask me. It's all a lot of talk.'

'Quite right. All an illusion,' Mr Severn agreed. 'A bottle of ginger ale,' he said to the waiter.

Heather said, 'We'll have to have a bottle of whisky. You don't mind, do you, dear?'

'Don't worry, child, don't worry,' Mr Severn said. 'It was only my little joke . . . a bottle of whisky,' he told the waiter.

'Will you pay now, if you please?' the waiter asked when he brought the bottle.

'What a price!' Maidie said, frowning boldly at the waiter. 'Never mind, by the time I've had a few goes at this I ought to have forgotten my troubles.'

Heather pinched up her lips. 'Very little for me.'

'Well, it's going to be drunk,' Mr Severn said. 'Play *Dinah*,' he shouted at the orchestra.

The saxophonist glanced at him and tittered. Nobody else took any notice.

'Sit down and have a drink, won't you?' Heather clutched at Mr Johnson's sleeve as he passed the table, but he answered loftily, 'Sorry, I'm afraid I can't just now,' and passed on.

'People are funny about drinking,' Maidie remarked. 'They get you to buy as much as they can and then afterwards they laugh at you behind your back for buying it. But on the other hand, if you try to get out of buying it, they're damned rude. Damned rude, they can be. I went into a place the other night where they have music – the International Café, they call it. I had a whisky and I drank it a bit quick because I was thirsty and feeling down and so on. Then I thought I'd like to listen to the music – they don't play so badly there because they say they're Hungarians – and a waiter came along, yelling "Last drinks". "Can I have some water?" I said. "I'm not here to serve you with water," he said. "This isn't a place to drink water in," he said, just like that. So loud! Everybody was staring at me.'

'Well, what do you expect?' Heather said. 'Asking for water! You haven't got any sense. No more for me, thank you.' She put her hand over her glass.

'Don't you trust me?' Mr Severn asked, leering.

'I don't trust anybody. For why? Because I don't want to be let down, that's why.'

'Sophisticated, she is,' said Maidie.

'I'd rather be sophisticated than a damned pushover like

you,' Heather retorted. 'You don't mind if I go and talk to some friends over there, do you, dear?'

'Admirable.' Mr Severn watched her cross the room. 'Admirable. Disdainful, debonair and with a touch of the tarbrush too, or I'm much mistaken. Just my type. One of my types. Why is it that she isn't quite – Now, why?' He took a yellow pencil out of his pocket and began to draw on the tablecloth.

Pictures, pictures, pictures. . . . Face, faces, faces. . . . Like hyaenas, like swine, like goats, like apes, like parrots. But not tigers, because tigers are better-looking, aren't they? as Hans says.

Maidie was saying, 'They've got an awfully nice "Ladies" here. I've been having a chat with the woman; she's a friend of mine. The window was open and the street looked so cool and peaceful. That's why I've been so long.'

'London is getting very odd, isn't it?' Mr Severn said in a thick voice. 'Do you see that tall female over there, the one in the backless evening gown? Of course, I've got my own theory about backless evening gowns, but this isn't the moment to tell you of it. Well, that sweetiepie's got to be at Brixton tomorrow morning at a quarter-past nine to give a music lesson. And her greatest ambition is to get a job as stewardess on a line running to South Africa.'

'Well, what's wrong with that?' Maidie said.

'Nothing – I just thought it was a bit mixed. Never mind. And do you see that couple over there at the bar? The lovely dark brown couple. Well, I went over to have a change of drinks and got into conversation with them. I rather palled up with the man, so I asked them to come and see me one day. When I gave them my address the girl said at once, "Is that in Mayfair?" "Good Lord, no; it's in the darkest, dingiest Bloomsbury." "I didn't come to London to go to the slums," she said with the most perfect British accent, high, sharp, clear and shattering. Then she turned her back on me and hauled the man off to the other end of the bar.'

'Girls always cotton on to things quicker,' Maidie asserted.

'The social climate of a place?' said Mr Severn. 'Yes, I suppose they do. But some men aren't so slow either. Well, well, tigers are better-looking, aren't they?'

'You haven't been doing too badly with the whisky, dear, have you?' Maidie said rather uneasily. 'What's all this about tigers?'

Mr Severn again addressed the orchestra in a loud voice. 'Play *Dinah*. I hate that bloody tune you keep playing. It's always the same one too. You can't fool me. Play *Dinah, is there anyone finer?* That's a good old tune.'

'I shouldn't shout so loud,' Maidie said. 'They don't like it here if you shout. Don't you see the way Johnson's looking at you?'

'Let him look.'

'Oh, do shut up. He's sending the waiter to us now.'

'Obscene drawings on the tablecloths not allowed here,' the waiter said as he approached.

'Go to hell,' Mr Severn said. 'What obscene drawings?'

Maidie nudged him and shook her head violently.

The waiter removed the tablecloth and brought a clean one. He pursed his lips up as he spread it and looked severely at Mr Severn. 'No drawings of any description on tablecloths are allowed here,' he said.

'I'll draw as much as I like,' Mr Severn said defiantly. And the next thing he knew two men had him by the collar and were pushing him towards the door.

'You let him alone,' said Maidie. 'He hasn't done anything. You are a lot of sugars.'

'Gently, gently,' said Mr Johnson, perspiring. 'What do you

want to be so rough for? I'm always telling you to do it quietly.'

As he was being hauled past the bar, Mr Severn saw Heather, her eyes beady with disapproval, her plump face lengthened into something twice the size of life. He made a hideous grimace at her.

'My Lawd,' she said, and averted her eyes. 'My Lawd!'

Only four men pushed them down the stairs, but when they were out in the street it looked more like fourteen, and all howling and booing. 'Now, who are all these people?' Mr Severn thought. Then someone hit him. The man who had hit him was exactly like the waiter who had changed the tablecloth. Mr Severn hit back as hard as he could and the waiter, if he was the waiter, staggered against the wall and toppled slowly to the ground. 'I've knocked him down,' Mr Severn thought. 'Knocked him down!'

'Tally-ho!' he yelled in a high voice. 'What price the tame grey mare?'

The waiter got up, hesitated, thought better of it, turned round and hit Maidie instead.

'Shut up, you bloody basket,' somebody said when she began to swear, and kicked her. Three men seized Mr Severn, ran him off the pavement and sprawled him in the middle of Wardour Street. He lay there, feeling sick, listening to Maidie. The lid was properly off there.

'Yah!' the crowd round her jeered. 'Boo!' Then it opened up, servile and respectful, to let two policemen pass.

'You big blanks,' Maidie yelled defiantly. 'You something somethings. I wasn't doing anything. That man knocked me down. How much does Johnson pay you every week for this?'

Mr Severn got up, still feeling very sick. He heard a voice: 'That's 'im. That's the chap. That's 'im what started everything.' Two policemen took him by the arms and marched him along. Maidie, also between two policemen, walked in front, weeping. As they passed through Piccadilly Circus, empty and desolate, she wailed, 'I've lost my shoe. I must stop and pick it up. I can't walk without it.'

The older policeman seemed to want to force her on, but the younger one stopped, picked the shoe up and gave it to her with a grin.

'What's she want to cry for?' Mr Severn thought. He shouted 'Hoi, Maidie, cheer up. Cheer up, Maidie.'

'None of that,' one of his policemen said.

But when they arrived at the police station she had stopped crying, he was glad to see. She powdered her face and began to argue with the sergeant behind the desk.

'You want to see a doctor, do you?' the sergeant said.

'I certainly do. It's a disgrace, a perfect disgrace.'

'And do you also want to see a doctor?' the sergeant asked, coldly polite, glancing at Mr Severn.

'Why not?' Mr Severn answered.

Maidie powdered her face again and shouted, 'God save Ireland. To hell with all dirty sneaks and Comic Cuts and what-have-yous.'

'That was my father speaking,' she said over her shoulder as she was led off.

As soon as Mr Severn was locked into a cell he lay down on the bunk and went to sleep. When they woke him to see the doctor he was cold sober.

'What time is it?' the doctor asked. With a clock over his head, the old fool!

Mr Severn answered coldly, 'A quarter-past four.'

'Walk straight ahead. Shut your eyes and stand on one leg,' the doctor demanded, and the policeman watching this performance sneered vaguely, like schoolboys when the master baits an unpopular one.

When he got back to his cell Mr Severn could not sleep. He lay down, stared at the lavatory seat and thought of the black eye he would have in the morning. Words and meaningless phrases still whirled tormentingly round in his head.

He read the inscriptions on the grim walls. 'Be sure your sins will find you out. B. Lewis.' 'Anne is a fine girl, one of the best, and I don't care who knows it. (Signed) Charlie S.' Somebody else had written up, 'Lord, save me; I perish.' and underneath, 'SOS, SOS, SOS (signed) G.R.'

'Appropriate,' Mr Severn thought, took his pencil from his pocket, wrote, 'SOS, SOS, SOS (Signed) N.S.,' and dated it.

Then he lay down with his face to the wall and saw, on a level with his eyes, the words, 'I died waiting'.

Sitting in the prison van before it started, he heard somebody whistling *The Londonderry Air* and a girl talking and joking with the policemen. She had a deep, soft voice. The appropriate adjective came at once into his mind – a sexy voice.

'Sex, sexy,' he thought. 'Ridiculous word! What a give-away!'

'What is wanted,' he decided, 'is a brand-new lot of words, words that will mean something. The only word that means anything now is death – and then it has to be my death. Your death doesn't mean much.'

The girl said, 'Ah, if I was a bird and had wings, I could fly away, couldn't I?'

'Might get shot as you went,' one of the policemen answered.

'This must be a dream,' Mr Severn thought. He listened for Maidie's voice, but there was not a sound of her. Then the van started.

It seemed a long way to Bow Street. As soon as they got out of the van he saw Maidie, looking as if she had spent the whole night in tears. She put her hand up to her hair apologetically.

'They took my handbag away. It's awful.'

'I wish it had been Heather,' Mr Severn thought. He tried to smile kindly.

'It'll soon be over now, we've only got to plead guilty.'

And it was over very quickly. The magistrate hardly looked at them, but for reasons of his own he fined them each thirty shillings, which entailed telephoning to a friend, getting the money sent by special messenger and an interminable wait.

It was half-past twelve when they were outside in Bow Street. Maidie stood hesitating, looking worse than ever in the yellowish, livid light. Mr Severn hailed a taxi and offered to take her home. It was the least he could do, he told himself. Also the most.

'Oh, your poor eye!' Maidie said. 'Does it hurt?'

'Not at all now. I feel astonishingly well. It must have been good whisky.'

She stared into the cracked mirror of her handbag.

'And don't I look terrible too? But it's no use; I can't do anything with my face when it's as bad as this.'

'I'm sorry.'

'Oh, well,' she said, 'I was feeling pretty bad on account of the way that chap knocked me down and kicked me, and afterwards on account of the way the doctor asked me my age. "This woman's very drunk," he said. But I wasn't, was I? . . . Well, and when I got back into the cell, the first thing I saw was my own name written up. My Christ, it did give me a turn! Gladys Reilly – that's my real name. Maidie Richards is only what I call myself. There it was staring me in the face. "Gladys Reilly, October 15th, 1934. . . ." Besides, I hate being locked up. Whenever I think of all these people they lock up for years I shiver all over.'

'Yes,' Mr Severn said, 'so do I.' *I died waiting.*

'I'd rather die quick, wouldn't you?'

'Yes.'

'I couldn't sleep and I kept on remembering the way the doctor said, "How old are you?" And all the policemen round were laughing, as if it was a joke. Why should it be such a joke. But they're hard up for jokes, aren't they? So when I got back I couldn't stop crying. And when I woke up I hadn't got my bag. The wardress lent me a comb. She wasn't so bad. But I do feel fed up. . . .'

'You know the room I was waiting in while you were telephoning for money?' she said. 'There was such a pretty girl there.'

'Was there?'

'Yes, a very dark girl. Rather like Dolores del Rio, only younger. But it isn't the pretty ones who get on – oh no, on the contrary. For instance, this girl. She couldn't have been prettier – lovely, she was. And she was dressed awfully nicely in a black coat and skirt and a lovely clean white blouse and a little white hat and lovely stockings and shoes. But she was frightened. She was so frightened that she was shaking all over. You saw somehow that she wasn't going to last it out. No, it isn't being pretty that does it. . . . And there was another one, with great hairy legs and no stockings, only sandals. I do think that when people have hairy legs they ought to wear stockings, don't you? Or do something about it. But no, she was just laughing and joking and you saw whatever happened to her she'd come out all right. A great big, red, square face she had, and those hairy legs. But she didn't care a damn.'

'Perhaps it's being sophisticated,' Mr Severn suggested, 'like your friend Heather.'

'Oh, her – no, she won't get on either. She's too ambitious, she wants too much. She's so sharp she cuts herself, as you might say. . . . No, it isn't being pretty and it isn't being sophisticated. It's being – adapted, that's what it is. And it isn't any good *wanting* to be adapted, you've got to be born adapted.'

'Very clear,' Mr Severn said. Adapted to the livid sky, the ugly houses, the grinning policemen, the placards in shop windows.

'You've got to be young, too. You've got to be young to enjoy a thing like this – younger than we are,' Maidie said as the taxi drew up.

Mr Severn stared at her, too shocked to be angry.

'Well, good-bye.'

'*Good*-bye,' said Mr Severn, giving her a black look and ignoring her outstretched hand. 'We' indeed!

Two hundred and ninety-six steps along Coptic Street. One hundred and twenty round the corner. Forty stairs up to his flat. A dozen inside it. He stopped counting.

His sitting-room looked well, he thought, in spite of the crumpled papers. It was one of its good times, when the light was just right, when all the incongruous colours and shapes became a whole – the yellow-white brick wall with several of the Museum pigeons perched on it, the silvered drainpipe, the chimneys of every fantastical shape, round, square, pointed, and the odd one with the mysterious hole in the middle through which the grey, steely sky looked at you, the solitary trees – all framed in the silver oilcloth curtains (Hans's idea), and then with a turn of his head he saw the woodcuts from Amsterdam, the chintz-covered arm-chairs, the fading bowl of flowers in the long mirror.

An old gentleman wearing a felt hat and carrying a walking-stick passed the window. He stopped, took off his hat and coat and, balancing the stick on the end of his nose, walked backwards and forwards, looking up expectantly. Nothing happened. Nobody thought him worth a penny. He put his hat and coat on again and, carrying the stick in a respectable manner, vanished round the corner. And, as he did so, the tormenting phrases vanished too – 'Who pays? Will you pay now, please? You don't mind if I leave you, dear? I died waiting, I died waiting. (Or was it I died hating?) That was my father speaking. Pictures, pictures, pictures. You've got to be young. But tigers are better-looking, aren't they? SOS, SOS, SOS. If I was a bird and had wings I could fly away, couldn't I? Might get shot as you went. But tigers are better-looking, aren't they? You've got to be younger than we are. . . .' Other phrases, suave and slick, took their place.

The swing's the thing, the cadence of the sentence. He had got it.

He looked at his eye in the mirror, then sat down at the typewriter and with great assurance rapped out 'JUBILEE. . . .'

Outside the Machine

I

THE big clinic near Versailles was run on strictly English lines, so every morning the patients in the women's general ward were woken up at six. They had tea and bread-and-butter. Then they lay and waited while the nurses brought tin basins and soap. When they had washed they lay and waited again.

There were fifteen beds in the tall, narrow room. The walls were painted grey. The windows were long but high up, so that you could see only the topmost branches of the trees in the grounds outside. Through the glass the sky had no colour.

At half-past ten the matron, attended by a sister, came in to inspect the ward, walking as though she were royalty opening a public building. She stopped every now and again, glanced at a patient's temperature chart here, said a few words there. The young woman in the last bed but one on the left-hand side was a newcomer. 'Best, Inez,' the chart said.

'You came last evening, didn't you?'

'Yes.'

'Quite comfortable?'

'Oh yes, quite.'

'Can't you do without all those things while you are here?'

the matron asked, meaning the rouge, powder, lipstick and hand mirror on the bed table.

'It's so that I shouldn't look too awful, because then I always feel much worse.'

But the matron shook her head and walked on without smiling, and Inez drew the sheets up to her chin, feeling bewildered and weak. *I'm cold, I'm tired.*

'Has anyone ever told you that you're very much like Raquel Meller?' the old lady in the next bed said. She was sitting up, wrapped in a black shawl embroidered with pink and yellow flowers.

'Am I? Oh, am I really?'

'Yes, very much like.'

'Do you think so?' Inez said.

The tune of *La Violetera*, Raquel Meller's song, started up in her head. She felt happier – then quite happy and rather gay. 'Why should I be so damned sad?' she thought. 'It's ridiculous. The day after I come out of this place something lucky might happen.'

And it was not so bad lying there and having everything done for you. It was only when you moved that you got frightened because you couldn't imagine ever moving again without hurting yourself.

She looked at the row of beds opposite and sighed. 'It's rum here, isn't it?'

'Oh, you'll feel different tomorrow,' the old lady said. She spoke English hesitatingly – not with an accent, but as if her tongue were used to another language.

The two talked a good deal that day, off and on.

'. . . And how was I to know,' Inez complained, 'that, on top of everything else, my inside would go *kaput* like this? And of course it must happen at the wrong time.'

'Now, shut up,' she told herself, 'shut up. Don't say, "Just when I haven't any money." Don't give yourself away. What a fool you are!' But she could not stop the flood of words.

At intervals the old lady clicked her tongue compassionately or said 'Poor child'. She had a broad, placid face. Her hair was black – surely dyed, Inez thought. She wore two rings with coloured stones on the third finger of her left hand and one – a thick gold ring carved into an indistinguishable pattern – on the little finger. There was something wrong with her knee, it appeared, and she had tried several other hospitals.

'French hospitals are more easy-going, but I was very lucky to get into this place; it has quite a reputation. There's nothing like English nursing. And, considering what you get, you pay hardly anything. An English matron, a resident English doctor, several of the nurses are English. I believe the private rooms are *most* luxurious, but of course they are very expensive.'

Her name was Tavernier. She had left England as a young girl and had never been back. She had been married twice. Her first husband was a bad man, her second husband was a good man. Just like that. Her second husband was a good man who had left her a little money.

When she talked about the first husband you could tell that she still hated him, after all those years. When she talked about the good one tears came into her eyes. She said that they were perfectly happy, completely happy, never an unkind word and tears came into her eyes.

'Poor old mutt,' Inez thought, 'she really has persuaded herself to believe that.'

Madame Tavernier said in a low voice, 'Do you know what he said in the last letter he wrote to me? "You are everything to me." Yes, that's what he said in the last letter I had.'

'Poor old mutt,' Inez thought again.

Madame Tavernier wiped her eyes. Her face looked calm

and gentle, as if she were repeating to herself, 'Nobody can say this isn't true, because I've got the letter and I can show it.'

The fat, fair woman in the bed opposite was also chatting with her neighbour. They were both blonde, very clean and aggressively respectable. For some reason they fitted in so well with their surroundings that they made everyone else seem dubious, out of place. The fat one discussed the weather, and her neighbour's answers were like an echo. 'Hot . . . oh yes, very hot . . . hotter than yesterday . . . yes, much hotter . . . I wish the weather would break . . . yes, I wish it would, but no chance of that . . . no, I suppose not . . . oh, I rather fancy so. . . .'

Under cover of this meaningless conversation the fair woman's stare at Inez was sharp, sly and inquisitive. 'An English person? English, what sort of English? To which of the seven divisions, sixty-nine subdivisions, and thousand-and-three subsubdivisions do you belong? (*But only one sauce, damn you.*) My world is a stable, decent world. If you withhold information, or if you confuse me by jumping from one category to another, I can be extremely disagreeable, and I am not without subtlety and inventive powers when I want to be disagreeable. Don't underrate me. I have set the machine in motion and crushed many like you. Many like you . . .'

Madame Tavernier shifted uneasily in her bed, as if she sensed this clash of personalities – stares meeting in mid-air, sparks flying. . . .

'Those two ladies just opposite are English,' she whispered.

'Oh, are they?'

'And so is the one in the bed on the other side of you.'

'The sleepy one they make such a fuss about?'

'She's a dancer – a "girl", you know. One of the Yetta Kauffman girls. She's had an operation for appendicitis.'

'Oh, has she?'

'The one with the screen round her bed,' Madame Tavernier chattered on, 'is very ill. She's not expected to – And the one . . .'

Inez interrupted after a while. 'They seem to have stuck all the English down this end, don't they? I wish they had mixed us up a bit more.'

'They never do,' Madame Tavernier answered. 'I've often noticed it.'

'It's a mistake,' said Inez. 'English people are usually pleasanter to foreigners than they are to each other.'

After a silence Madame Tavernier inquired politely, 'Have you travelled a lot?'

'Oh, a bit.'

'And do you like it here?'

'Yes, I like Paris much the best.'

'I suppose you feel at home,' Madame Tavernier said. Her voice was ironical. 'Like many people. There's something for every taste.'

'No, I don't feel particularly at home. That's not why I like it.'

She turned away and shut her eyes. She knew the pain was going to start again. And, sure enough, it did. They gave her an injection and she went to sleep.

Next morning she woke feeling dazed. She lay and watched two nurses charging about, very brisk and busy and silent. They did not even say 'Come along', or 'Now, now', or 'Drink that up.'

They moved about surely and quickly. They did everything in an impersonal way. They were like parts of a machine, she thought, that was working smoothly. The women in the beds bobbed up and down and in and out. They too were parts of a machine. They had a strength, a certainty, because all their lives they had belonged to the machine and worked smoothly, in and out, just as they were told. Even if the machine got out of control, even if it went mad, they would still work in and out, just as they were told, whirling smoothly, faster and faster, to destruction.

She lay very still, so that nobody should know she was afraid. Because she was outside the machine they might come along any time with a pair of huge iron tongs and pick her up and put her on the rubbish heap, and there she would lie and rot. 'Useless, this one,' they would say; and throw her away before she could explain, 'It isn't like you think it is, not at all. It isn't like they say it is. Wait a bit and let me explain. You must listen; it's very important.'

But in the evening she felt better.

The girl in the bed on the right, who was sitting up, said she wanted to write to a friend at the theatre.

'In French,' she said. 'Can anybody write the letter for me, because I don't know French?'

'I'll write it for you,' Madame Tavernier offered.

' "Dear Lili . . . L-i-l-i. Dear Lili . . ." well, say: "I'm getting all right again. Come and see me on Monday or Thursday. Any time from two to four. And when you come will you bring me some notepaper and stamps? I hope it won't be long before I get out of this place. I'll tell you about that on Monday. Don't forget the stamps. Tell the others that they can come to see me, and tell them how to get here. Your affectionate friend, and so on, Pat." Give it to me and I'll sign it. . . . Thanks.'

The girl's voice had two sounds in it. One was clear and light, the other heavy and ruthless.

'You seem to be having a rotten time, you in the next bed,' she said.

'I feel better now.'

'Have you been in Paris long?'

'I live here.'

'Ah, then you'll be having your pals along to cheer you up.'

'I don't think so. I don't expect anybody.'

The girl stared. She was not much over twenty and her clear blue eyes slanted upwards a little. She looked as if, standing up, she would be short with sturdy dancer's legs. Stocky, like a little pony.

Oh God, let her go on talking about herself and not looking at me, or sizing me up, or anything like that.

'This French girl, this friend of mine, she's a perfect scream,' Pat said. 'But she's an awfully obliging girl. If I say, "Turn up with stamps," she will turn up with stamps. That's why I'm writing to her and not to one of our lot. Our lot might turn up or they might not. You know. But she's a perfect scream, really. . . . As a matter of fact, she's not bad-looking, but the way she walks is too funny. She's a *femme nue*, and they've taught her to walk like that. It's all right without shoes, but with shoes it's – well . . . you'll see when she comes here. They only get paid half what we do, too. Anyway, she's an awfully obliging kid; she's a sweet kid, poor devil.'

A nurse brought in supper.

'The girls are nice and the actors are nice,' Pat went on, 'but the stage hands hate us. Isn't it funny? You see, one of them tried to kiss one of our lot and she smacked his face. He looked sort of surprised, she said. And then do you know what he did? He hit her back! Well, and do you know what we did? We said to the stage manager, "If that man doesn't get the sack, we won't go on." They tried one show without us and then they gave in. The principals whose numbers were spoilt made a hell of a row. The French girls can't do our stuff because they can't keep together. They're all right alone – very good sometimes, but they don't understand team work. . . . And now, my God, the stage hands don't half hate us. We have to go in twos to the lavatory. And yet, the girls and the actors are awfully nice; it's only the stage hands who hate us.'

The fat woman opposite – her name was Mrs Wilson – listened to all this, at first suspiciously, then approvingly. Yes, this is permissible; it has its uses. Pretty English chorus girl – north country – with a happy, independent disposition and bright, teasing eyes. Placed! All correct.

Pat finished eating and then went off to sleep again very suddenly, like a child.

'A saucy girl, isn't she?' Madame Tavernier said. Her eyes were half-shut, the corners of her mouth turned downwards.

Through the windows the light turned from dim yellow to mauve, from mauve to grey, from grey to black. Then it was dark except for the unshaded bulbs tinted red all along the ward. Inez put her arm round her head and turned her face to the pillow.

'Good night,' the old lady said. And after a long while she said, 'Don't cry, don't cry.'

Inez whispered, 'They kill you so slowly. . . .'

The ward was a long, grey river; the beds were ships in a mist. . . .

The next day was Sunday. Even through those window panes the sky looked blue, and the sun made patterns on the highly polished floor. The patients had breakfast half an hour later – seven instead of half-past six.

'Only milk for you today,' the nurse said. Inez was going to ask why; then she remembered that her operation was fixed for Monday. *Don't think of it yet. There's still quite a long time to go.*

After the midday meal the matron told them that an English clergyman was going to visit the ward and hold a short service if nobody minded. Nobody did mind, and after a while the parson came in through an unsuspected door, looking as if he felt very cold, as if he had never been warm in his life. He had grey hair and a shy, shut-in face.

He stood at the end of the ward and the patients turned their heads to look at him. The screen round the bed on the other side had been taken away and the yellow-faced, shrunken woman who lay there turned her head like the others and looked.

The clergyman said a prayer and most of the patients said 'Amen'. ('Amen,' they said. 'We are listening,' they said. . . . I am poor bewildered unhappy comfort me I am dying console me of course I don't let on that I know I'm dying but I know I know Don't talk about life as it is because it has nothing to do with me now Say something go on say something because I'm so darned sick of women's voices Christ how I hate women Say something funny that I can laugh at but anything you say will be funny you old geezer you Never mind say something . . . 'We are listening,' they said, 'we are listening. . . .') But the parson was determined to stick to life as it is, for his address was a warning against those vices which would antagonize their fellows and make things worse for them. Self-pity, for instance. Where does that lead you? Ah, where? Cynicism. So cheap. . . . Rebellion. So useless. . . . 'Let us remember,' he ended, 'that God is a just God and that man, made in His image, is also just. On the whole. And so, dear sisters, let us try to live useful, righteous and God-fearing lives in that state to which it has pleased Him to call us. Amen.'

He said another prayer and then went round shaking hands. 'How do you do, how do you do, how do you do?' All along the two lines. Then he went out again.

After he had gone there was silence in the ward for a few seconds, then somebody sighed.

Madame Tavernier remarked, 'Poor little man, he was so nervous.'

'Well, it didn't last long, anyway,' Pat said. 'On and off like the Demon King. . . .'

She began to sing:

> *'Oh, he doesn't look much like a lover,*
> *But you can't tell a book by its cover.'*

Then she sang *The Sheik of Araby*. She tied a towel round her head for a turban and began again: 'Over the desert wild and free . . . Sing up, girls, chorus. I'm the Sheik of Arabee. . . .'

Everybody looked at Pat and laughed; the dying woman's small yellow face was convulsed with laughter.

'There's lots of time before tomorrow,' Inez thought. 'I needn't bother about it yet.'

'I'm the Sheik of Arabee. . . .' Somebody was singing it in French – '*Je cherche Antinéa*.' It was a curious translation – significant when you came to think of it.

Pat shouted, 'Listen to this. Anybody recognize it? Old but good. "Who's that knocking at my door? said the fair young ladye. . . ." '

The tall English sister came in. She had a narrow face, small deep-set eyes of an unusual reddish-brown colour and a large mouth. Her pale lips lay calmly one on the other, as if she were very good-tempered, or perhaps very self-controlled. She smiled blandly and said, 'Now then, Pat, you must stop this,' arranged the screen round the bed on the other side and pulled down the blind of the window at the back.

It was really very hot and after she had gone out again most of the women lay in a coma, but Pat went on talking. The sound of her own voice seemed to excite her. She became emphatic, as if someone was arguing with her.

She talked about love and the difference between glamour and dirt. The real difference was £–s–d, she said. If there was some money about there could be some glamour; otherwise, say what you liked, it was simply dirty – as well as foolish.

'Plenty of survival value there,' Inez thought. She lay with her eyes closed, trying to see trees and smooth water. But the pictures she made slipped through her mind too quickly, so that they became distorted and malignant.

That night everybody in the ward was wakeful. Somebody moaned. The nurse rushed about with a bed pan, grumbling under her breath.

II

At nine o'clock on Monday morning the tall English sister was saying, 'You'll be quite all right. I'm going to give you a morphine injection now.'

After this Inez was still frightened, but in a much duller way.

'I hope you'll be there,' she said drowsily. But there was another nurse in the operating room. She was wearing a mask and she looked horrible, Inez thought – like a torturer.

Floating in the air, which was easy and natural after the morphine – *Of course, I've always been able to do this. Why did I ever forget? How stupid of me!* – she watched herself walking across the floor with tears streaming down her cheeks, supported by the terrifying stranger.

'Now, don't be silly,' the nurse said irritably.

Inez sat down on the edge of the couch, not floating now, not divided. One, and heavy as lead.

'You don't know why I'm crying,' she thought.

She tried to look at the sky, but there was a mist before her eyes and she could not see it. She felt hands pressing hard on her shoulders.

'No, no, no, leave her alone,' somebody said in French.

The English doctor was not there – only this man, who was also wearing a mask.

'They're so stupid,' Inez said in a high, complaining voice. 'It's terrible. Oh, what's going to happen, what's going to happen?'

'Don't be afraid,' the doctor said. His brown eyes looked kind. 'N'ayez pas peur, n'ayez pas peur.'

'All right,' Inez said, and lay down.

The English doctor's voice said, 'Now breathe deeply. Count slowly. One – two – three – four – five – six. . . .'

III

'Do you feel better today?' the old lady asked.

'Yes, much better.'

The blind at the back of her bed was down. It tapped a bit. She was sleepy; she felt as if she could sleep for weeks.

'Hullo,' said Pat, 'come to life again?'

'I'm much better now.'

'You've been awfully bad,' Pat said. 'You were awfully ill on Monday, weren't you?'

'Yes, I suppose I was.'

The screen which had been up round her bed for three days had shut her away even from her hand mirror; and now she took it up and looked at herself as if she were looking at a stranger. She had lain seeing nothing but a succession of pictures of the past, always sinister, always too highly coloured, always distorted. She had heard nothing but the incoherent, interminable conversations in her head.

'I look different,' she thought.

'I look awful,' she thought, staring anxiously at her thin, grey face and the hollows under her eyes. This was very important; her principal asset was threatened.

'I must rest,' she thought. 'Rest, not worry.'

She passed her powder puff over her face and put some rouge on.

Pat was watching her. 'D'you know what I've noticed? People who look ghastly oughtn't to put make up on. You only look worse if you aren't all right underneath – much older. My pal Lili came along on Monday. You should have seen how pretty she looked. I will say for these Paris girls they do know how to make up. . . .'

Yap, yap, yap. . . .

'Even if they aren't anything much – and often they aren't, mind you – they know how to make themselves look all right. I mean, you see prettier girls in London, but in my opinion. . . .'

The screen round the bed on the opposite side had been taken away. The bed was empty. Inez looked at it and said nothing. Madame Tavernier, who saw her looking at it, also said nothing, but for a moment her eyes were frightened.

IV

The next day the ward sister brought in some English novels.

'You'll find these very soothing,' she said, and there was a twinkle in her eye. A splendid nurse, that one; she knew her job. What they call a born nurse.

A born nurse, as they say. Or you could be a born cook, or a born clown or a born fool, a born this, a born that . . .

'What's the joke now?' Pat asked suspiciously.

'Oh, nothing. I was thinking how hard it is to believe in free will.'

'I suppose you know what you're talking about,' Pat answered coldly. She had become hostile for some reason. Not that it mattered. . . .

'Everything will be all right; I needn't worry,' Inez assured herself. 'There's still heaps of time.'

And soon she believed it. Lying there, being looked after and waking obediently at dawn, she began to feel like a child, as if the future would surely be pleasant, though it was hardly conceivable. It was as if she had always lain there and had known everyone else in the ward all her life – Madame Tavernier, her shawl, her rings, her crochet and her travel books, Pat and her repertoire of songs, the two fair, fat women who always looked so sanctimonious when they washed.

The room was wide and the beds widely spaced, but now she knew something of the others too. There was a mysterious girl with long plaits and a sullen face who sometimes helped the nurse to make the beds in the morning – mysterious because there did not seem to be anything the matter with her. She ought to have been pretty, but she always kept her head down and if by chance you met her eyes she would blink and glance away. And there was the one who wore luxury pyjamas, the one who knitted, the other constant reader – watching her was sometimes a frightening game – the one who had a great many visitors, the ugly one, rather like a monkey, who all day sewed something that looked like a pink crêpe-de-chine chemise.

But her dreams were uneasy, and if a book fell or a door banged her heart would jump – a painful echo. And she found herself disliking some of the novels the sister brought. One day when she was reading her face reddened with anger. *Why, it's not a bit like that. My Lord, what liars these people are! And nobody to stand up and tell them so. Yah, Judas! Thinks it's the truth! You're telling me.*

She glanced sideways. Pat, who was staring at her, laughed, raised her eyebrows and tapped her forehead. Inez laughed back, also tapped her forehead and a moment afterwards was reading again, peacefully.

The days were like that, but when night came she burrowed into the middle of the earth to sleep. 'Never wake up, never wake up,' her wise heart told her. But the morning always came, the tin basins, the smell of soap, the long, sunlit, monotonous day.

At last she was well enough to walk into the bathroom by herself. Going there was all right, but coming back her legs gave way and she had to put her hand on the wall of the passage for support. There was a weight round the middle of her body which was dragging her to earth.

She got back into bed again. Darkness, quiet, safety – all the same, it was time to face up to things, to arrange them neatly. 'One, I feel much worse than I expected: two, I must ask the matron tomorrow if I can stay for another week; they won't want me to pay in advance; three, as soon as I know that I'm all right for another week, I must start writing round and trying to raise some money. Fifty francs when I get out! What's fifty francs when you feel like this?'

That night she lay awake for a long time, making plans. But next morning, when the matron came round, she became nervous of a refusal. 'I'll ask her tomorrow for certain.' However, the whole of the next day passed and she did not say a word.

She ate and slept and read soothing English novels about the respectable and the respected and she did not say a word nor write a letter. Any excuse was good enough: 'She doesn't look in a good temper today. . . . Oh, the doctor's with her; I don't think he liked me much. (Well, I don't like you much either, old cock; your eyes are too close together.) Today's

Friday, not my lucky day. . . . I'll write when my head is clearer. . . .'

A long brown passage smelling of turpentine led from the ward to the washroom. There were rows of basins along either whitewashed wall, three water closets and two bathrooms at the far end.

Inez went to one of the washbasins. She was carrying a sponge bag. She took out of it soap, a toothbrush, toothpaste and peroxide.

Somebody opened the door stealthily, hesitated for a moment, then walked past and stood over one of the basins at the far end. It was the sullen girl, the one with the long plaits. She was wearing a blue kimono.

'She does look fed up,' Inez thought.

The girl leant over the basin with both hands on its edge. Was she going to be sick? Then she gave a long, shivering sigh and opened her sponge bag.

Inez turned away without speaking and began to clean her teeth.

The door opened again and a nurse came in and glanced round the washroom. It was curious to see the expression on her plump, pink face change in a few moments from indifference to inquisitiveness, to astonishment, to shocked anger.

Then she ran across the room, shouting, 'Stop that. Come along, Mrs Murphy. Give it up.'

Inez watched them struggling. Something metallic fell to the floor. Mrs Murphy was twisting like a snake.

'Come on, help me, can't you? Hold her arms,' the nurse said breathlessly.

'Oh, leave me alone, leave me alone,' Mrs Murphy wailed. 'Do for God's sake leave me alone. What do you know about it anyway?'

'Go and call the sister. She's in the ward.'

'She's speaking to me,' Inez thought.

'Oh, leave me alone, leave me alone. Oh, please, please, please, please, please,' Mrs Murphy sobbed.

'What's she done?' Inez said. 'Why don't you leave her alone?'

As she spoke two other nurses rushed in at the door and flung themselves on Mrs Murphy, who began to scream loudly, with her mouth open and her head back.

Inez held on to the basins, one by one, and got to the door. Then she held on to the door post, then to the wall of the passage. She reached her bed and lay down shaking.

'What's up? What's the matter?' Pat asked excitedly.

'I don't know.'

'Was it Murphy? You're all right, aren't you? We were wondering if it was Murphy, or . . .'

' "Or you," she means,' Inez thought. ' "Or you . . ." '

All that evening Pat and the fair woman, Mrs Wilson, who had become very friendly, talked excitedly. It seemed that they knew all about Mrs Murphy. They knew that she had tried the same thing on before. Suddenly, by magic, they seemed to know all about her. And what a thing to do, to try to kill yourself! If it had been a man, now, you might have been a bit sorry. You might have said, 'Perhaps the poor devil has had a rotten time.' But a woman!

'A married woman with two sweet little kiddies.'

'The fool,' said Pat. 'My God, what would you do with a fool like that?'

Mrs Wilson, who had been in the clinic for some time, explained that there was a medicine cupboard just outside the ward.

'It must have been open,' she said. 'In *which* case, somebody will get into a row. Perhaps Murphy got hold of the key. That's where she might get the morphine tablets.'

But Pat was of the opinion – she said she knew it for a fact, a nurse had told her – that Mrs Murphy had had the hypodermic syringe and the tablets hidden for weeks, ever since she had been in the clinic.

'She's one of these idiotic neurasthenics, neurotics, or whatever you call them. She says she's frightened of life, I ask you. That's why she's here. Under observation. And it only shows you how cunning they are, that she managed to hide the things. . . .'

'I'm so awfully sorry for her husband,' said Mrs Wilson. 'And her children. So sorry. The poor kiddies, the poor sweet little kiddies. . . . Oughtn't a woman like that to be hung?'

Even after the lights had been put out they still talked.

'What's she got to be neurasthenic and neurotic about, anyway?' Pat demanded. 'If she has a perfectly good husband and kiddies, what's she got to be neurasthenic and neurotic about?'

Stone and iron, their voices were. One was stone and one was iron. . . .

Inez interrupted the duet in a tremulous voice. 'Oh, she's neurasthenic, and they've sent her to a place like this to be cured? That was a swell idea. What a place for a cure for neurasthenia! Who thought that up? The perfectly good, kind husband, I suppose.'

Pat said, 'For God's sake! You get on my nerves. Stop always trying to be different from everybody else.'

'Who's everybody else?'

Nobody answered her.

'What a herd of swine they are!' she thought, but no heat of rage came to warm or comfort her. Sized her up, Pat had. *Why should you care about a girl like that? She's as stupid as a foot. But not when it comes to sizing people up, not when it comes to knowing who is done for. I'm cold, I'm tired, I'm tired, I'm cold.*

The next morning Mrs Murphy appeared in time to help make the beds. As usual she walked with her head down and her eyes down and her shoulders stooped. She went very slowly along the opposite side of the ward, and everybody stared at her with hard, inquisitive eyes.

'What are you muttering about, Inez?' Pat said sharply.

Mrs Murphy and the nurse reached the end of the row opposite. Then they began the other row. Slowly they were coming nearer.

'Shut up, it's nothing to do with you,' Inez told herself, but her cold hands were clenched under the sheet.

The nurse said, 'Pat, you're well enough to give a hand, aren't you? I won't be a moment.'

'Idiot,' Inez thought. 'She oughtn't to have gone away. But they never know what's happening. But yes, they know. The machine works smoothly, that's all.'

In silence Pat and Mrs Murphy started pulling and stretching and patting the sheets and pillows.

'Hullo, Pat,' Mrs Murphy said at last in a low voice.

Pat closed her lips with a righteously disgusted expression.

They turned the sheet under at the bottom. They smoothed it down at the top. They began to shake the pillows.

Mrs Murphy's face broke up and she started to cry. 'Oh God,' she said, 'they won't let me get out. They won't.'

Pat said, 'Don't snivel over my pillow. People like you make me sick,' and Mrs Wilson laughed like a horse neighing.

The voice and the laughter were so much alike that they might have belonged to the same person. *Greasy and cold, silly and raw, coarse and thin; everything unutterably horrible.*

'Well, here's bad luck to you,' Inez burst out, 'you pair of bitches. Behaving like that to a sad woman! What do you know about her? . . . You hold your head up and curse them back, Mrs Murphy. It'll do you a lot of good.'

Mrs Murphy rushed out of the room sobbing.

'Who was speaking to you?' Pat said.

Inez heard words coming round and full and satisfying out of her mouth – exactly what she thought about them, exactly what they were, exactly what she hoped would happen to them.

'Disgusting,' said Mrs Wilson. 'I *told* you so,' she added triumphantly. 'I knew it, I knew the sort she was from the first.'

At this moment the door opened and the doctor came in accompanied, not as usual by the matron, but by the tall ward sister.

Once more, for a gesture, Inez shouted, 'This and that to the lot of you!' – 'Not the nurse,' she whispered to the pillow, 'I don't mean her.'

Mrs Wilson announced in a loud, clear voice, 'I think that people who use filthy language oughtn't to be allowed to associate with decent people. I think it's a shame that some women are allowed to associate with ladies at all – a shame. It oughtn't to be allowed.'

The doctor blinked, but the sister's long, narrow face was expressionless. The two went round the beds glancing at the temperature charts here, saying a few words there. Best, Inez . . .

The doctor asked, 'Does this hurt you?'

'No.'

'When I press here does it hurt you?'

'No.'

They were very tall, thin and far away. They turned their heads a little and she could not hear what they said. And when she began, 'I wanted to . . .' she saw that they could not hear her either, and stopped.

V

'You can dress in the washroom after lunch,' the sister said next morning.

'Oh, yes?'

There was nothing to be surprised about. So much time had been paid for and now the time was up and she would have to go. There was nothing to be surprised about.

Inez said, 'Would it be possible to stay two or three days longer? I wanted to make some arrangements. It would be more convenient. I was idiotic not to speak about it before.'

The sister's raised eyebrows were very thin – like two thin new moons.

She said, 'I'm sorry, I'm afraid it's not possible. Why didn't you ask before? I told the doctor yesterday that I don't think you are very strong yet. But we are expecting four patients this evening and several others tomorrow afternoon. Unfortunately we are going to be very full up and he thinks you are well enough to go. You must rest when you get back home. Move as little as possible.'

'Yes, of course,' Inez said; but she thought, 'No, this time I won't be able to pull it off, this time I'm done.' '*We wondered if it was Murphy – or you. . . .' Well, it's both of us.*

Then her body relaxed and she lay and did not think of anything, for there is peace in despair in exactly the same way as there is despair in peace. Everything in her body relaxed. She did not make any more plans, she just lay there.

They had their midday dinner – roast beef, potatoes and beans, and then a milk pudding. Just like England. Inez ate and enjoyed it, and then lay back with her arm over her eyes. She knew that Pat was watching her but she lay still, peaceful, and thought of nothing.

'Here are your things,' the nurse said. 'Will you get dressed now?'

'All right.'

'I'm afraid you're not feeling up to much. Well, you'll have some tea before you go, won't you? And you must go straight to bed as soon as you get back.'

'Get back where?' Inez thought. 'Why should you always take it for granted that everybody has somewhere to get back to?'

'Oh yes,' she said, 'I will.'

And all the time she dressed she saw the street, the 'buses and taxis charging at her, the people jostling her. She heard their voices, saw their eyes. . . . When you fall you don't ever get up; they take care of that. . . .

She leant against the wall thinking of Mrs Murphy's voice when she said, 'Please, please, please, please, please. . . .'

After a while she wiped the tears off her face. She did not put any powder on, and when she got into the ward she could only see the bed she was going to lie on and wait till they came with the tongs to throw her out.

'Will you come over here for a moment?'

There was a chair at the head of each bed. She sat down and looked at the fan-shaped wrinkles under Madame Tavernier's small, dark, melancholy eyes, the swollen blue veins on her hands and the pattern of the gold ring – two roses, the petals touching each other. She read a sentence of the open book lying on the bed: 'De là-haut le paysage qu'on découvre est d'une indescriptible beauté . . .'

Madame Tavernier said, 'That's a charming dress, and you look very nice – very nice indeed.'

'My God!' Inez said. 'That's funny.'

Madame Tavernier whispered, 'S-sh, listen! Turn the chair round. I want to talk to you.'

Inez turned the chair so that her back was towards the rest of the room.

Madame Tavernier took a handkerchief from under her pillow – a white, old-fashioned handkerchief, not small, of very fine linen trimmed with lace. She put it into Inez' hands. 'Here,' she said. 'S-sh . . . here!'

Inez took the handkerchief. It smelt of vanilla. She felt the notes inside it.

'Take care. Don't let the others see. Don't let them notice you crying. . . .' She whispered, 'You mustn't mind these people; they don't know anything about life. You mustn't mind them. So many people don't know anything about life . . . so many of them . . . and sometimes I wonder if it isn't getting worse instead of better.' She sighed. 'You hadn't any money, had you?'

Inez shook her head.

'I thought you hadn't. There's enough there for a week or perhaps two. If you are careful.'

'Yes, yes,' Inez said. 'Now I'll be quite all right.'

She stopped crying. She felt tired, rested and rather degraded. She had never taken money from a woman before. She did not like women, she had always told herself, or trust them.

Madame Tavernier went on talking. 'That is quite a lot of money if you use it carefully,' she meant. But that was not what she said.

'Thank you,' Inez said, 'oh, thank you.'

'You'd like some tea before you go, wouldn't you?' the nurse said.

Inez drank the tea, went into the washroom and made up her face. She went back to the old lady's bed.

'Will you give me a kiss?' Madame Tavernier said.

Her powdered skin was soft and flabby as used elastic; it

smelt, like her handkerchief, of vanilla. When Inez said, 'I'll never forget your kindness, it's made such a difference to me,' she closed her eyes in a way that meant, 'All right, all right, all right.'

'I'll have a taxi to the station,' Inez decided.

But in the taxi she could only wonder what Madame Tavernier would say if she were suddenly asked what it is like to be old – perhaps she would answer, 'Sometimes it's peaceful' – and remember the gold ring carved into two roses, and above all wish she were back in her bed in the ward with the sheets drawn over her head. Because you can't die and come to life again for a few hundred francs. It takes more than that. It takes more, perhaps, than anybody is ever willing to give.

The Lotus

'GARLAND says she's a tart.'

'A tart! My dear Christine, have you seen her? After all, there are limits.'

'What, round about the Portobello Road? I very much doubt it.'

'Nonsense,' Ronnie said. 'She's writing a novel. Yes, dearie – ' he opened his eyes very wide and turned the corners of his mouth down – 'all about a girl who gets seduced – '

'Well, well.'

'On a haystack.' Ronnie roared with laughter.

'Perhaps we'll have a bit of luck; she may get tight earlier than usual tonight and not turn up.'

'Not turn up? You bet she will.'

Christine said, 'I can't imagine why you asked her here at all.'

'Well, she borrowed a book the other day, and she said she was coming up to return it. What was I to do?'

While they were still arguing there was a knock on the door and he called, 'Come in. . . . Christine, this is Mrs Heath, Lotus Heath.'

'Good evening,' Lotus said in a hoarse voice. 'How are you? Quite well, I hope. . . . Good evening, Mr Miles. I've brought your book. *Most* enjoyable.'

She was a middle-aged woman, short and stout. Her plump arms were bare, the finger nails varnished bright red. She had rouged her mouth unskilfully to match her nails, but her face was very pale. The front of her black dress was grey with powder.

'The way these windows rattle!' Christine said. 'Hysterical, I call it.' She wedged a piece of newspaper into the sash, then sat down on the divan. Lotus immediately moved over to her side and leaned forward.

'You do like me, dear, don't you? Say you like me.'

'Of course I do.'

'I think it's so nice of you to ask me up here,' Lotus said. Her sad eyes, set very wide apart, rolled vaguely round the room, which was distempered yellow and decorated with steamship posters – 'Morocco, Land of Sunshine,' 'Come to Beautiful Bali'. 'I get fed up, I can tell you, sitting by myself in that basement night after night. And day after day too if it comes to that.'

Christine remarked primly, 'This is a horribly depressing part of London, I always think.'

Her nostrils dilated. Then she pressed her arms close against her sides, edged away and lit a cigarette, breathing the smoke in deeply.

'But you've got it very nice up here, haven't you? Is that a photograph of your father on the mantelpiece? You are like him.'

Ronnie glanced at his wife and coughed. 'Well, how's the poetry going?' he asked, smiling slyly as he said the word 'poetry' as if at an improper joke. 'And the novel, how's that getting on?'

'Not too fast,' Lotus said, looking at the whisky decanter. Ronnie got up hospitably.

She took the glass he handed to her, screwed up her eyes, emptied it at a gulp and watched him refill it with an absent-minded expression.

'But it's wonderful the way it comes to me,' she said. 'It's going to be a long book. I'm going to get everything in – the whole damn thing. I'm going to write a book like nobody's ever written before.'

'You're quite right, Mrs Heath, make it a long book,' Ronnie advised.

His politely interested expression annoyed Christine. 'Is he trying to be funny?' she thought, and felt prickles of irritation all over her body. She got up, murmuring, 'I'll see if there's any more whisky. It's sure to be needed.'

'The awful thing,' Lotus said as she was going out, 'is not knowing the words. That's the torture – knowing the thing and not knowing the words.'

In the bedroom next door Christine could still hear her monotonous, sing-song voice, the voice of a woman who often talked to herself. 'Springing this ghastly old creature on me!' she thought. 'Ronnie must be mad.'

'This place is getting me down,' she thought. The front door was painted a bland blue. There were four small brass plates and bell-pushes on the right-hand side – Mr and Mrs Garland, Mr and Mrs Miles, Mrs Spencer, Miss Reid, and a dirty visiting-card tacked underneath – Mrs Lotus Heath. A painted finger pointed downwards.

Christine powdered her face and made up her mouth carefully. What could the fool be talking about?

'Is it as hopeless as all that?' she said, when she opened the sitting-room door. Lotus was in tears.

'Very good.' Ronnie looked bashful and shuffled his feet.

'Very good indeed, but a bit sad. Really, a bit on the sad side, don't you think?'

Christine laughed softly.

'That's what my friend told me,' Lotus said, ignoring her hostess. ' "Whatever you do, don't be gloomy," he said, "because that gets on people's nerves. And don't write about anything you know, for then you get excited and say too much, and that gets under their skins too. Make it up; use your imagination." And what about my book? That isn't sad, is it? I'm using my imagination. All the same, I wish I could write down some of the things that have happened to me, just write them down straight, sad or not sad. I've had my bit of fun too; I'll say I have.'

Ronnie looked at Christine, but instead of responding she looked away and pushed the decanter across the table.

'Have another drink before you tell us any more. Do, please. That's what the whisky's here for. Make the most of it, because I'm sorry to say there isn't any more in the kitchen and the pub is shut now.'

'She thinks I'm drinking too much of your Scotch,' Lotus said to Ronnie.

'No, I'm sure she doesn't think that.'

'Well, don't think that, dear – what's your name? – Christine. I've got a bottle of port downstairs and I'll go and get it in a minute.'

'Do,' Christine said. 'Let's be really matey.'

'That's right, dear. Well, as I was saying to Mr Miles, the best thing I ever wrote was poetry. I don't give a damn about the novel, just between you and me. Only to make some money, the novel is. Poetry's what I really like. All the same, the memory I've got, you wouldn't believe. Do you know, I can remember things people have said to me ever so long ago? If I try, I can hear the words and I can remember the voice saying them. It's wonderful, the memory I've got. Of course, I can't do it as well now as I used to, but there you are, nobody stays young for ever.'

'No, isn't it distressing?' Christine remarked to no one in particular. 'Most people go on living long after they ought to be dead, don't they? Especially women.'

'Sarcastic, isn't she? A dainty little thing, but sarcastic.' Lotus got up, swayed and held on to the mantelpiece. 'Are you a mother, dear?'

'Do you mean me?'

'No, I can see you're not – and never will be if you can help it. You're too fly, aren't you? Well, anyway, I've just finished a poem. I wrote it with the tears running down my face and it's the best thing I ever wrote. It was as if somebody was saying into my ears all the time, "Write it, write it." Just like that. It's about a woman and she's in court and she hears the judge condemning her son to death. "You must die," he says. "No, no, no," the woman says, "he's too young." But the old judge keeps on. "Till you die," he says. And, you see–' her voice rose – 'he's not real. He's a dummy, like one of those things ventriloquists have, he's not *real*. And nobody knows it. But she knows it. And so she says – wait, I'll recite it to you.'

She walked into the middle of the room and stood very straight, with her head thrown back and her feet together. Then she clasped her hands loosely behind her back and announced in a high, artificial voice, 'The Convict's Mother.'

Christine began to laugh. 'This is too funny. You mustn't think me rude, I can't help it. Recitations always make me behave badly.' She went to the gramophone and turned over the records. 'Dance for us instead. I'm sure you dance beautifully. Here's the very thing – *Just One More Chance*. That'll do, won't it?'

'Don't take any notice of her,' Ronnie said. 'You go on with the poem.'

'Not much I won't. What's the good, if your wife doesn't like poetry?'

'Oh, she's only a silly kid.'

'Tell me what you laugh at, and I'll tell you what you are,' Lotus said. 'Most people laugh when you're unhappy, that's when they laugh. I've lived long enough to know that – and maybe I'll live long enough to see them laugh the other side of their faces, too.'

'Don't you take any notice of her,' Ronnie repeated. 'She's like that.' He nodded at Christine's back, speaking in a proud and tender voice. 'She was telling me only this morning that she doesn't believe in being sentimental about other people. Weren't you, Christine?'

'I didn't tell you anything of the sort.' Christine turned round, her face scarlet. 'I said I was tired of slop – that's what I said. And I said I was sick of being asked to pity people who are only getting what they deserve. When people have a rotten time you can bet it's their own fault.'

'Go on,' said Lotus. 'You're talking like a bloody fool, dear. You've never felt anything in your life, or you wouldn't be able to say that. Rudimentary heart, that's your trouble. Your father may be a clergyman, but you've got a rudimentary heart all the same.' She was still standing in the middle of the room, with her hands behind her back. 'You tell her, Mr What's-your-name? Tell the truth and shame the devil. Go on, tell your little friend she's talking like a bloody fool.'

'Now, now, now, what's all this about?' Ronnie shifted uncomfortably. He reached out for the decanter and tilted it upside down into his glass. 'It's always when you want a drink really badly that there isn't any more. Have you ever noticed it? What about that port?'

The two women were glaring at each other. Neither answered him.

'What about that port, Mrs Heath? Let's have a look at that port you promised us.'

'Oh yes, the port,' Lotus said, 'the port. All right, I'll get it.'

As soon as she had gone Christine began to walk up and down the room furiously. 'What's the idea? Why are you encouraging that horrible woman? "Your little friend," did you hear that? Does she think I'm your concubine or something? Do you like her to insult me?'

'Oh, don't be silly, she didn't mean to insult you,' Ronnie argued. 'She's tight – that's what's the matter with her. I think she's damned comic. She's the funniest old relic of the past I've struck for a long time.'

Christine went on as if she had not heard him. 'This hellish, filthy slum and my hellish life in it! And now you must produce this creature, who stinks of whisky and all the rest better left unsaid, to *talk* to me. To talk to me! There are limits, as you said yourself, there are limits. . . . Seduced on a haystack, my God! . . . She oughtn't to be touched with a barge-pole.'

'I say, look out,' Ronnie said. 'She's coming back. She'll hear you.'

'Let her hear me,' said Christine.

She went on to the landing and stood there. When she saw the top of Lotus' head she said in a clear, high voice, 'I really can't stay any longer in the same room as that woman. The mixture of whisky and mustiness is too awful.'

She went into the bedroom, sat down on the bed and began to laugh. Soon she was laughing so heartily that she had to put the back of her hand over her mouth to stop the noise.

'Hullo,' Ronnie said, 'so here you are.'

'I couldn't find the port.'

'That's all right. Don't you worry about that.'

'I did have some.'

'That's quite all right. . . . My wife's not very well. She's had to go to bed.'

'I know when I've had the bird, Mr Miles,' Lotus said. 'Only give us another drink. I bet you've got some put away somewhere.'

There was some sherry in the cupboard.

'Thanks muchly.'

'Won't you sit down?'

'No, I'm going. But see me downstairs. It's so dark, and I don't know where the lights are.'

'Certainly, certainly.'

He went ahead, turning on the lights at each landing, and she followed him, holding on to the banisters.

Outside, the rain had stopped but the wind was still blowing strong and very cold.

'Help me down these damned steps, will you? I don't feel too good.'

He put his hand under her arm and they went down the area steps. She got her key out of her bag and opened the door of the basement flat.

'Come on in for a minute. I've got a lovely fire going.'

The room was small and crowded with furniture. Four straight-backed chairs with rococo legs, armchairs with the stuffing coming out, piles of old magazines, photographs of Lotus herself, always in elaborate evening dress, smiling and lifeless.

Ronnie stood rocking himself from heel to toe. He liked the photographs. 'Must have been a good-looking girl twenty years ago,' he thought, and as if in answer Lotus said in a tearful voice, 'I had everything; my God, I had. Eyes, hair, teeth, figure, the whole damned thing. And what was the good of it?'

The window was shut and a brown curtain was drawn across it. The room was full of the sour smell of the three dustbins that stood in the area outside.

'What d'you pay for this place?' Ronnie said, stroking his chin.

'Thirty bob a week, unfurnished.'

'Do you know that woman owns four houses along this street? And every floor let, basements and all. But there you are – money makes money, and if you haven't any you can whistle for it. Yes, money makes money.'

'Let it,' said Lotus. 'I don't care a damn.'

'Now then, don't talk so wildly.'

'I don't care a damn. Tell the world I said it. Not a damn. That was never what I wanted. I don't care about the things you care about.'

'Cracked, poor old soul,' he thought, and said: 'Well, I'll be getting along if you're all right.'

'You know – that port. I really had some. I wouldn't have told you I had some if I hadn't. I'm not that sort of person at all. You believe me, don't you?'

'Of course I do.' He patted her shoulder. 'Don't you worry about a little thing like that.'

'When I came down it had gone. And I don't need anybody to tell me where it went, either.'

'Ah?'

'Some people are blighters; some people are proper blighters. He takes everything he can lay his hands on. Never comes to see me except it's to grab something.' She put her elbows on her knees and her head in her hands and began to cry. 'I've had enough. I've had enough, I can tell you. The things people say! My Christ, the things they say. . . .'

'Oh, don't let them get you down,' Ronnie said. 'That'll never do. Better luck next time.'

She did not answer or look at him. He fidgeted. 'Well, I must be running along, I'm afraid. Cheerio. Remember – better luck next time.'

As soon as he got upstairs Christine called out from the bedroom, and when he went in she told him that they must get away, that it wasn't any good saying he couldn't afford a better flat, he must afford a better flat.

Ronnie thought that on the whole she was right, but she talked and talked and after a while it got on his nerves. So he went back into the sitting-room and read a list of second-hand gramophone records for sale at a shop near by, underlining the titles that attracted him. *I'm a Dreamer, Aren't We All? I've Got You Under My Skin* – that one certainly; he underlined it twice. Then he collected the glasses and took them into the kitchen for the charwoman to wash up the next morning.

He opened the window and looked out at the wet street. 'I've got you under my skin,' he hummed softly.

The street was dark as a country lane, bordered with lopped trees. It glistened – rather wickedly, he thought.

'Deep in the heart of me,' he hummed. Then he shivered – a very cold wind for the time of year – turned away from the window and wrote a note to the charwoman: 'Mrs Bryan. Please call me as soon as you get here.' He underlined 'soon' and propped the envelope up against one of the dirty dishes. As he did so he heard an odd, squeaking noise. He looked out of the window again. A white figure was rushing up the street, looking very small and strange in the darkness.

'But she's got nothing on,' he said aloud, and craned out eagerly.

A police whistle sounded. The squeaking continued, and the Garlands' window above him went up.

Two policemen half-supported, half-dragged Lotus along. One of them had wrapped her in his cape, which hung down to her knees. Her legs were moving unsteadily below it. The trio went down the area steps.

Christine had come into the kitchen and was looking over his shoulder. 'Good Lord,' she said. 'Well, that's one way of attracting attention if all else fails.'

The bell rang.

'It's one of the policemen,' said Ronnie.

'What's he want to ring our bell for? We don't know anything about her. Why doesn't he ring somebody else's bell?'

The bell rang again.

'I'd better go down,' Ronnie said.

'Do you know anything about Mrs Heath, Mrs Lotus Heath, who lives in the basement flat?' the policeman asked.

'I know her by sight,' Ronnie answered cautiously.

'She's a bit of a mess,' said the policeman.

'Oh, dear!'

'She's passed out stone cold,' the policeman went on confidentially. 'And she looks as if there's something more than drink the matter, if you ask me.'

Ronnie said in a shocked voice – he did not know why – 'Is she dying?'

'Dying? No!' said the policeman, and when he said 'No!' death became unthinkable, the invention of hysteria, something that simply didn't happen. Not to ordinary people. 'She'll be all right. There'll be an ambulance here in a minute. Do you know anything about the person?'

'Nothing,' Ronnie said, 'nothing.'

'Ah?' The policeman wrote in his notebook. 'Is there anybody else in the house, do you think, who'd give us some information?' He shone a light on the brass plates on the door post. 'Mr Garland?'

'Not Mr Garland,' Ronnie answered hurriedly. 'I'm sure not. She's not at all friendly with the Garlands, I know that for a fact. She didn't have much to do with anybody.'

'Thank you very much,' the policeman said. Was his voice ironical?

He pressed Miss Reid's bell and when no answer came looked upwards darkly. But he didn't get any change out of Number Six, Albion Crescent. Everybody had put their lights out and shut their windows.

'You see – ' Ronnie began.

'Yes, I see,' the policeman said.

When Ronnie got upstairs again Christine was in bed.

'Well, what was it all about?'

'She seems to have conked out. They're getting an ambulance.'

'Really? Poor devil.' ('Poor devil' she said, but it did not mean anything.) 'I thought she looked awful, didn't you? That dead-white face, and her lips such a funny colour after her lipstick got rubbed off. Did you notice?'

A car stopped outside and Ronnie saw the procession coming up the area steps, everybody looking very solemn and important. And it was pretty slick, too – the way they put the stretcher into the ambulance. He knew that the Garlands were watching from the top floor and Mrs Spencer from the floor below. Miss Reid's floor was in darkness because she was away for a few days.

'Funny how this street gives me goose-flesh tonight,' he thought. 'Somebody walking over my grave, as they say.'

He could not help admiring the way Christine ignored the whole sordid affair, lying there with her eyes shut and the eiderdown pulled up under her chin, smiling a little. She looked very pretty, warm and happy like a child when you have given it a sweet to suck. And peaceful.

A lovely child. So lovely that he had to tell her how lovely she was, and start kissing her.

A Solid House

I

'WHAT's happening now?' Miss Spearman said loudly. She was very deaf.

'A bit quieter,' Teresa shouted.

Miss Spearman put her hands to her ears and shook her head. She hadn't heard.

'There, love,' she said. Her arms were thin as drum-sticks, her chest bony, her hair soft as a cat's fur. 'It's all over. There, love.'

'Cigarette?' Teresa said.

But when she opened her cigarette case it was empty. That was because the tobacconist on the corner had refused to sell her any the evening before. He always refused women customers when there was a shortage – and very pleased he was to be able to do it. She wondered what the old beast would say if he knew that she rather liked him. His open hatred and contempt were a relief from all the secret hatreds that hissed from between the lines of newspapers or the covers of books, or peeped from sly smiling eyes. A woman? Yes, a woman. A woman must, a woman shall or a woman will. . . .

Miss Spearman was fussing about something, too.

'I've left my earphone upstairs. Stupid! D'you think it's worth-while going to get it?'

'No, don't. Better not,' Teresa said. Certainly better not, she thought, as the silence and emptiness gradually filled with fragments of sentences, columns of figures which she was compelled to add up, subtract and multiply – and with the sound of that first scream and crash. The top of her head, which felt very thin anyway, began to rattle and shake.

Miss Spearman said, whispering this time, 'Right overhead now, aren't they? Perhaps they're ours.'

Ours? Perhaps, maybe . . .

Pressed flat against the cellar wall, they listened to the inexorable throbbing of the planes. And above them the house waited, its long, gloomy passages full of echoes, shadows, creakings – rats, perhaps. But the square outside was calm and indifferent, the trees cleaner than in a London square, not smelling the same, either.

'Anything?' Miss Spearman asked.

'Gone, I think,' Teresa said, and made signs.

She remembered playing hide-and-seek in a cellar very like this one long ago. Curious, that hide-and-seek. It started well. You picked your side (I pick you, I pick you), then suddenly, in the middle, something happened. Everything changed and became horrible and meaningless. But still it went on. You hid, or you ran with a red face, pretending you knew what it was all about. The boys showed off, became brutal; the girls trotted along, imitating, trying to keep up, but with sidelong looks, sudden fits of giggling, which often ended in tears.

'Well,' Miss Spearman said peevishly, 'what are they waiting for? Why don't they hurry up with the All Clear?'

Teresa smiled and shrugged her shoulders. 'They've gone,' she thought, soothed. 'Gone home to get their medals pinned on, gone home to get something to eat.' She had got used to the cellar, she did not want to leave it now. Why leave this good, this perfectly safe, windowless cellar, so like that other long ago?

'Nothing changes much,' she thought, remembering the bellowed orders, contradicted the next minute – Left turn. No, right turn. No, as you were, silly ass – the obligatory grin, the idiotic jokes, repeated over and over again, which you had to laugh at, at first unwillingly, then so hysterically that your jaws ached, and the endless arguments as to whether the girls might carry knives slung to their waists or not. 'Oh, the girls can't have knives.' 'Why not?' 'Well, because they aren't officers. The girls are only common sailors.' 'Yes, but common sailors do have knives,' said Norman, the soft one, the one who liked girls, you suspected. 'That's the great thing about being a common sailor.' At last it was decided that the leader of the girls could have a knife, the others could carry sticks. The worst part of this horrible game came when the frenzy was over and the damage done. Then the boys would cluster in a group, and one of them would be sure to say, 'It was the girls' fault. They started it; they egged us on. They were worse than we were.'

'Well,' she said, 'there you are. That'll be all for this morning.'

Miss Spearman did not answer. She stared straight ahead, strained, listening.

'The All Clear,' Teresa said, speaking carefully. Now she could think again, she could tell herself, 'Don't shout. Pitch your voice right and she'll hear.'

'Ah!' said Miss Spearman. 'Not much of a raid.' Her expression changed, became spiteful. 'You are nervy, aren't you? Look at your hand shaking.'

'It's so cold down here.'

'Come along then. We'll have something to warm us up.'

They went up the steep stone stairs, past the brass gong in

the hall, the brass tray for visiting cards, the dim looking glass, malevolent with age, into the kitchen.

II

The kitchen was a large, comfortable room. The owner of the house had gone off when the raids started, to live at an hotel in the Lake District. ('People said she oughtn't to have done it – that it was a bad example. But when they get to that age what can you expect? "They can't stand the racket these devils make when they're her age," I said.') Miss Spearman, who looked like an ex-lady's maid, or housekeeper, perhaps, or poor relation or half-acknowledged relation – there must be some half-acknowledged relations knocking around, even in this holy and blessed isle – was installed and let rooms to select lodgers.

She lit the fire, talking about air raids, land mines and slaughter.

'Why, there wasn't a pane of glass left in the square. Everything down, from St Agnes's to the County Tea Shop. That *was* a night.'

She went into the scullery and came back with tea and bread-and-butter on a black lacquer tray.

'I'll have mine later; I like it strong. I must go and see if my blind old lady's all right.' She said the words 'old lady' in a patronizing, pitying and scornful tone. 'And then perhaps Olly Pearce at Number Seven may have heard the news.'

There were two red plush armchairs near the fire, a patchwork rug, a calendar with a picture of cats, a round table with a wool mat in the middle, a large black cupboard and, on the walls, some old prints of soldiers in full dress – Ensign of His Majesty's Dragoon Guards, Captain of the 78th Foot – fellows of those in Captain Roper's bedroom upstairs, which

Teresa always imagined looked down at him so approvingly as he slept. 'Sleep on, chum,' they said. 'Snore well, mate.'

Captain Roper, her fellow lodger, was away on a course. And a very good thing too, for he had turned against her now, and she knew perfectly well why.

On the first night of her stay they had gone together to the nearest cinema. After dinner on the second night they had settled down by the fire – he in the big armchair, she in the smaller one – and he had produced a half bottle of whisky.

'Have a spot?'

'Battledress doesn't do justice to a man's figure,' he said after the second whisky, and it probably didn't to his. He had a small, handsome, cocky, ageless face and a cocky little moustache.

He told her that he thought things were going to be very difficult after this war – worse than the last, which was bad enough. In 1920 he had been in Mexico, but in 1921 he was back in London. On his uppers. 'Pop went everything except my dress suit. In 1914. . . .'

'But you must have been very young in 1914,' Teresa said flatteringly.

Captain Roper blinked. 'Well, as a matter of fact I was. However, I remember. . . .'

Yes, pre-war 1914 must have been a golden time.

Teresa stopped listening. When she next heard what he was saying he was no longer in 1914; he was in 1924, giving lessons in Mah Jong to keep body and soul together.

'And some very interesting pupils I had too. I taught Mah Jong to the prettiest woman I've ever seen. Lovely young creature – dark, very vivacious. She got rather bored with it, of course. Scoring too complicated.' His hard, shallow, sentimental eyes looked past her. Perhaps he saw a sunny street and trim steps up to a freshly painted door and flower boxes in the windows and the decorative, unattainable young creature in the room inside. 'I can't remember her name. A double-barrelled name. It's on the tip of my tongue.'

Double-barrelled names raced through Teresa's brain.

'Ah, I've remembered it,' Captain Roper said. 'Barton-Lumley.'

'Barton-Lumley?'

'Yes, Mrs Barton-Lumley. She got bored,' he muttered, and, after a pause, 'She died.'

Then Teresa had laughed loudly. One of those terrible laughs which now shook her at the most unexpected moments. It came from the depths of her – a real devil of a laugh. Every time this happened she would think 'Who's that laughing?'

She smoothed her face and tried to turn it into a cough.

'Oh, what a shame! Beautiful people oughtn't to die; they ought to be guarded and protected and kept alive, whoever else dies. There are so few of them.'

But this was useless. He looked at her with distrust – and he had gone on looking at her with distrust.

'No,' she was thinking when Miss Spearman came back, 'I'll never know the rest of the story – what happened in 1925 or 1938, in 1927 or 1931. . . .'

'Norton Street,' Miss Spearman said, pouring out her tea, 'and I hear they've got Bailey's.'

'Pretty close. That must have been that first bang.'

'Yes. Olly says she's heard that fifteen people were killed, but old Jimmy says thirty. If it's Norton Street, we can go and have a look this afternoon. But it's no use going now, do you think? Well, you seem better already,' she went on. 'You looked very bad in the cellar, I thought, as white as a – as white as a sheet. You mustn't let your nerves get on top of you, you know. It doesn't do. Think of something else. You want a bit of cheering up.'

She walked across the room and opened a cupboard, which was full of dresses, underclothes, sandals, brassieres, kimonos – ladies' second-hand clothes, Miss Spearman's sideline.

'What about this? Three and sixpence.'

She held up a brown felt halo hat with a long veil attached to it.

'Wouldn't I look comic in that?' Teresa said. 'Well, I mean, a bit comic?'

'Yes, perhaps it's not quite your style,' Miss Spearman agreed. She was now wearing her earphone and it seemed to be working perfectly. 'Well, what about this costume? I only got it yesterday. Very smart woman she is – wears some lovely clothes. She wants two pounds for it. Just been cleaned. I'll let you have it for thirty shillings.'

'But I don't like that shade of green. I don't like green at all. It's not my lucky colour.'

'What?' Miss Spearman said. 'I can't hear you. Take it into your room and try it on. A pound to you – and that's giving it away.'

'All right,' Teresa said feebly. She took the hideous thing and hung it at the back of her chair. She thought, 'Yes, I'll end by buying it, and I'll end by walking about in it too, God help me.'

Then she recognized her own black dress in the cupboard. It was hanging next to a shapeless purple coat. A cast-off self, it stared back so forlornly, so threateningly that she turned her eyes away.

'Have another cup,' Miss Spearman said. 'I see you're looking at your old black. I hope to get it off this week. But you can't expect much.'

'No, I suppose not.'

'Black's too depressing. Twelve and six I might get.'

'Well, it cost me quite a lot, you know.'

'Yes, I know it's well cut, but it's a depressing dress all the same. Would you take ten bob?'

Her face looked very sharp and eager, her brown eyes glittered. You wouldn't have thought she was talking about shillings at all.

'If that's all I can get. . . .'

Miss Spearman relaxed.

'Funny how tired these air raids make you, isn't it?' she said, sighing. 'It's afterwards you feel it, I always think. Yes, it's afterwards you feel it.'

'Sit still. I'll wash the cups up,' Teresa said.

But the scullery was like the cellar – dim and dark, with only one small window high up to light the sink, the rusty gas-stove, the stupid moon-faced plates in the rack, the cheerful cups, the gloomy saucepans on hooks. So she was glad to come back into the kitchen, where Miss Spearman was talking to herself about the charwoman.

'I'm sure Nelly won't turn up. I'm sure she'll make this raid an excuse. She always does. Most annoying. And they never go anywhere near the part she lives in.'

'I don't know what the working class is coming to. Haven't you noticed it?' she said. 'And this house is too much for me without any help, officers or no officers.'

'And,' she continued, 'I do it for love, as you might say. How will they manage when people like me are dead and gone? They'll soon find out what it's like.' Something in her mournful and complaining voice made you see all the houses growing dustier, dingier, more silent. 'What's to happen if everything's left to go to rack and ruin?' she lamented. 'Where do they expect people to live? In underground caves, or in concrete barracks, or what?'

'Some will,' said Teresa, 'and some, as they say, will not.'

Don't worry, everything will survive somewhere – the

polished floors, the bowls of roses, the scented hair, the painted nails. Some will sink, but others will swim. Trust Bibi. . . .

She put her hand over her eyes, which felt sore, and listening to the noisy clock, thought about that other clock ticking so slowly, the watch on the table ticking so fast. But the same seconds, or they said the same seconds. Not that she believed a word they said.

'I know she isn't coming. An hour and a half late now. The whole trouble is that they promise things that they don't mean to do. It's very un-English, very. And she was going to cut the cards for me today, too. She's wonderful at that, I will say.'

She clasped and unclasped her hands in her lap. They were very red and raw, the joints swollen – the only ungraceful things about her.

'Miss Spearman, I admire you so much.'

'Do you?'

'Yes, and I envy you.'

'Envy me?' Miss Spearman said happily. She looked into the little glass over the mantelpiece. 'I never touch my hair or my face with anything but rain water. From that cask outside. Soft water – that's the secret.'

Teresa said, 'Yes – your appearance, of course. But what I meant was that I admire you because you're always so calm, so sure of yourself, and because. . . .'

It was a glittering, glaring day outside, the sky blown blue. A heartless, early spring day – acid, like an unripe gooseberry. There was a cold, yellow light on the paved garden and the tidy, empty flower beds and on the high wall, where a ginger cat sat staring at birds. You could see his neat paw-marks in the damp mould.

'I feel so well,' Teresa said, 'though a bit sleepy. That shows

I'm getting better – feeling well so early in the morning before the break of day. Almost.'

'Have you been ill?' Miss Spearman asked inquisitively. 'A lot of people are feeling it now, a lot of people. Of course, not these young, heartless people.'

Teresa said, 'Do you think young people are heartless? Aren't old people heartless? And people who are getting old – aren't they heartless too?'

'I can see you've been ill. I can see it in your eyes.'

'Oh, nothing much,' said Teresa.

But instead of turning her head away she looked straight at Miss Spearman – straight into a hard, bright glitter, hard and bright as the day outside. But behind the glitter there was surely something nebulous, dreamy, soft? Usually the sweetness and softness, if any, was displayed for all to see; but, hidden away, what continents of distrust, what icy seas of silence. Voyage to the Arctic regions. . . .

She thought, 'Shall I tell her about it on this fresh, new morning?'

III

But then it was afternoon – a hot afternoon. You know, there does come an afternoon when you think 'I want a rest; I want a good long sleep'. So I took two tablets, and then another two. Then I drank some whisky and it seemed quite clear. Now, my lass, now Hope, the vulture, will have to go and feed on somebody else. I thought, 'I must wear my pretty dress for this.' So I went upstairs and put on my blue dress and powdered my face. I didn't hurry, but when I came down again the hands of the clock hadn't moved at all. Which shows that it's true, what they say: 'Time is made for slaves.' Then I knew I must do it and so I swallowed all the tablets in the bottle with the whisky.

Seven grains each they were – strong. And I saw some spilt on the floor. 'I must take these too,' I thought. But before I could take them I don't remember anything more.

When I woke up the first thing I saw was the blue dress on the chair. And the doctor was there. 'What are you doing here?' I said, and he answered, 'It's the afternoon I always come to see you.' So I knew it was Tuesday. A whole night and a day gone, and I shall never know what happened. And afterwards too I don't remember. I had dreams, of course. But were they dreams? . . .

She said, 'I liked this house as soon as I saw it. And you seemed exactly right when you opened the door. Not the sort of person who goes all of a doodah, like me.'

'It's a lovely old house,' Miss Spearman said. 'Solid.'

'Yes, lovely and solid,' Teresa said.

But how can you tell? The other one was solid, too. As you approached it the river, which had been narrow, broadened out, like an avenue, straight, with willows on each bank. The water was covered with dead leaves. The paddle did not make any sound, the dead leaves slowed the punt down. Round a corner was the house – turrets and gables and balconies and green shutters all mixed up. It looked empty and dilapidated. The boards of the landing-stage were broken and rotten. Two statues faced one another – the gentleman wore a cocked hat, knee-breeches and tail-coat, but the lady showed a large breast. She held up her draperies with one hand, the other was raised as if she were listening. The lawn was dark green and smooth and in the middle was a cedar tree. The rocking-horse under it was painted white with red spots. There wasn't a sound. And I knew that if I could pass the statues and touch the tree and walk into the house, I should be well again. But they wouldn't let me do that, the simple thing that always makes you well.

How much shall I tell her? Shall I tell her that in spite of everything they did I died then? Shall I tell her what it feels like to be dead? It's not being sad, it's quite different. It's being nothing, feeling nothing. You don't feel insults, you wouldn't feel caresses if there was anyone to caress you. It's like this – it's like walking along a road in a fog, knowing that you have left everything behind you. But you don't want to go back; you've got to go on. There are moments when you know where you are going, but then you forget and you walk on, torturing yourself, trying to remember, for it's very important. When you start, you often look back to catch them laughing or making faces in the bright lights away from the fog. Later on you don't do that; you don't care any longer. If they were to laugh until their mouths met at the back and the tops of their heads fell off like some loathsome over-ripe fruit – as they doubtless will one day – you wouldn't turn your head to see the horrible but comic sight. . . .

'Yes, I've been ill,' she said. 'I've been having a holiday. I was staying not so far from here and I saw your advertisement in the local paper.'

Miss Spearman said, 'I usually let my rooms to officers. But this happened to be a slack time.'

Teresa smiled. 'Lucky for me.'

How much have I told her? What have I said. . . .

Not too much, for Miss Spearman did not seem to be at all surprised.

'Calm?' she said. 'Of course, it's better to be calm. I don't believe in hysteria. Not for women, anyhow. Sometimes a man can get away with hysteria, but not a woman. And then of course don't be too much alone. People don't like it. The things they say if you're alone! You have to have a good deal of money to get away with that. And keep up with your friends. Write letters. And a good laugh always helps, of course.'

'Which helps most – with or at?'

'I don't quite follow you,' Miss Spearman said. 'And then a little bit of gossip.'

. . . See people. Write letters. Join the noble and gallant army of witch-hunters – both sexes, all ages eligible – so eagerly tracking down some poor devil, snouts to the ground. Watch the witch-hunting, witch-pricking ancestor peeping out of those close-set Nordic baby-blues.

But are you telling me the real secret, how to be exactly like everybody else? Tell me, for I am sure you know. If it means being deaf, then I'll be deaf. And if it means being blind, then I'll be blind. I'm afraid of that road, Miss Spearman – the one that leads to madness and to death, they say. That's not true. It's longer than that. But it's a terrible road to put your feet on, and I'm not strong enough; let somebody else try it. I want to go back. Tell me how to get back; tell me what to do and I'll do it.

'And then,' Miss Spearman said, 'there's another thing. . . .'

Teresa leaned forward eagerly.

'Olly Pearce,' Miss Spearman said in a low mysterious voice, 'is a medium.'

'A what? . . . Oh, I see.'

'We have sittings, sometimes at her place, sometimes here, sometimes at Mrs Davis's. I've had messages, and I hear them at night, just before I sleep. Especially since I've grown so deaf. It always starts with a humming, twanging noise in my head.'

'Yes, that's how it starts, isn't it?' Teresa said, staring at her.

'Was that the bell?' Miss Spearman sat very erect. 'It's that slut Nelly. Excuse the word. Over two hours late.'

She went out into the hall, and Nelly could be heard, loudly explaining, arguing, and then becoming aggressive. And Miss

Spearman's shrill answers, which ended on a high, thin note.

She came back into the kitchen, looking triumphant.

'Well, what are you going to do while your room's being turned out? Why not go for a little walk to Norton Street, and see what's to be seen?'

'No, I don't think I will,' Teresa said. In Norton Street a doll, or a dressmaker's dummy, would stare blankly, a cigarette poster, untouched, flapping in the wind, would smile, beckon, wave a coy finger. The notice would say, 'Danger: No Thoroughfare.'

She heard Nelly outside, shovelling coal violently into a scuttle.

'Why, the old badger!' said Nelly, 'the bloody old. . . .'

The radio next door began to sing defiantly 'Now's the time for Paradise, Paradise for two. . . .'

IV

'I generally keep it locked,' Miss Spearman said. 'But I open it up and air it and light a fire every Tuesday.'

'And it's Tuesday today, of course,' Teresa thought. 'Always Tuesday. . . .'

'Captain Roper sits in here sometimes,' Miss Spearman said, 'so why shouldn't you?'

She led the way through the white-painted door into another room – a long, narrow, pathetic room. Gold brocade curtains shut out the square, but the windows which led into the garden were open. There was a freshly lighted fire, no dust sheets – everything was spick and span.

'Aren't they beautiful?' Miss Spearman said, pointing to a case of stuffed birds, neatly labelled in careful, slanting handwriting. There was a card in the corner, in the same writing:

'I believe in the Resurrection of the Dead.' A fanatic bird-lover? A joke? Or had Miss Spearman picked it up and put it there to preserve the admirable sentiment?

Teresa came close and looked at the birds which would rise again – White Heron, Lapwing, Great Crested Grebe, Indian Cock Pheasant, Wild Duck and, in a corner, four humming birds. Four humming birds with fierce glass eyes.

'Well, you've grown up now, haven't you?' she said to them. 'You are having your own back.'

Miss Spearman was talking about the pictures in white or faded gold frames which covered the walls. Pictures of blue seas – but not too blue, not a vulgar, tropical blue – of white walls – but not stark – of shadows – but not too black. Pictures of gentlemen with powdered hair and ladies with ringlets falling on long, graceful necks, their mouths mournful, patient or smiling as the case might be. One was holding a violin, another a book.

There was a mirror in a silver-green frame, and glass paper-weights through which could be seen roses, carnations and violets. There were white jade vases, and the Woolworth's glass mats they were standing on were as touching as Miss Spearman's red hands or make up used by an ageing woman. ('Must make the best of the poor old face.')

'Perhaps there's a musical box,' Teresa thought. 'Perhaps it will play "Pink and blue, pink and blue, Do you know what love can do? Love can kill. . . ." '

There was no musical box, but there were Japanese wind-glasses, again from Woolworth's, hanging over the door into the garden.

'You say you're tired,' Miss Spearman said. 'Why not lie down and have a little rest? Have a little doze. The sofa's quite comfortable.' And left her.

She recognized one of the gentlemen now – the one with

china-blue eyes – also the lady with the violin. There were portraits of them in her room, but here they hung straight, with no string visible, with no incongruous text between them – 'The Lord is my Shepherd, and I shall lack nothing.'

She sat down on a gilt chair and saw that there was a small bookshelf behind a red and gold screen, the only gaudy thing in the room. And the right books were in it – *The Heart of Rome*, *Wanda*, *All for the Czar*, *As a Dream When One Awaketh*, *From One Generation to Another*. 'Yes, this is paradise,' she thought, and leant forward to touch the books. But next to innocent *Wanda* was a warning – *No Orchids for Miss Blandish*. 'I bet old Cap Roper brought that in here. Not that I've got anything against the book. On the contrary, didn't I win a quid ages ago when I bet that it was written by an Englishman, judging entirely by internal evidence and confounding the experts?'

She began to walk restlessly up and down the room, thinking, 'No, if I slept here I'd dream. I'd dream of monstrous humming birds, cellars, flowers under glass, gentlemen with china-blue eyes, ladies with smooth shoulders who will never lack the still pastures and the green waters, the peaceful death, the honoured grave – all this, and Heaven too – who will never, never lack the sense of superiority nor the disciplined reaction nor the proper way to snub nor the heart like a rock nor the wrist surprisingly thick. Nor the flower of the flock to be sacrificed.'

'I must find somewhere else to sleep,' she thought.

And then Miss Spearman opened the door and called 'Ready'.

V

In the dining-room the glass cases round the walls were full of shepherds and shepherdesses, mandarins and small china portrait figures.

'My sister brought me some new laid eggs yesterday. I do my best for you.'

'You do indeed.'

There were two newspapers by the plate, one unfamiliar, and when Miss Spearman came in to clear away the meal she hovered.

'Did you notice that paper? Very good, I think.'

'Yes, awfully good.'

But Miss Spearman did not seem satisfied with this response, or she had not heard it.

'You see,' she said, taking up the paper and pointing to an article marked with two red lines, 'it's all quite simple and homely – anyhow at the start. Many people simply won't believe they are dead, he says. He says it's quite amusing, if one may use the word.'

'If one may use the word.'

'Of course, it gets more complicated later on.'

'It always does get more complicated later on, don't you think?' Teresa said.

'We're going to try to sit tonight,' Miss Spearman said. 'We always get very good results after a raid. One learns not to question these things. Would you care to join us? Olly Pearce, Mrs Davis, myself and the lady who keeps the wool shop in Modder Street.'

'No,' Teresa said, 'no. I'm sorry I can't.'

'I'll think about it,' she said, laughing feebly. 'Like the green suit, I'll think about it.'

Although she was wearing her earphone Miss Spearman looked so bewildered that Teresa repeated, 'No. Not yet.'

'Of course,' Miss Spearman said stiffly, 'people mustn't be forced; they must come of their own free will. Just as you like.'

Her friendliness seemed to float away in the act of putting the dishes on the tray and she slammed the door so violently that the pictures on the walls and the little figures in the cases trembled.

But silence came and patched up the rent. Olly Pearce's young niece, wearing a blue overall, was in the front garden of Number Seven. She pushed her hair off her forehead, stretched, yawned. She was sleepy too. The ginger cat danced in the cold wind outside – three little steps one way, three little steps the other, backwards and spring.

Teresa lay down on the sofa and shut her eyes. The sound of the crash in her head became fainter. It was off on its journey, off on its travels, for ever and ever, world without end.

'My little doze,' she thought. 'At last. My little sleep.'

The Sound of the River

THE electric bulb hung on a short flex from the middle of the ceiling, and there was not enough light to read so they lay in bed and talked. The night air pushed out the curtains and came through the open window soft and moist.

'But what are you afraid of? How do you mean afraid?'

She said, 'I mean afraid like when you want to swallow and you can't.'

'All the time?'

'Nearly all the time.'

'My dear, really. You are an idiot.'

'Yes, I know.'

Not about this, she thought, not about this.

'It's only a mood,' she said. 'It'll go.'

'You're so inconsistent. You chose this place and wanted to come here, I thought you approved of it.'

'I do. I approve of the moor and the loneliness and the whole set-up, especially the loneliness. I just wish it would stop raining occasionally.'

'Loneliness is all very well,' he said, 'but it needs fine weather.'

'Perhaps it will be fine tomorrow.'

If I could put it into words it might go, she was thinking. Sometimes you can put it into words – almost – and so get rid of it – almost. Sometimes you can tell yourself I'll admit I was afraid today. I was afraid of the sleek smooth faces, the rat faces, the way they laughed in the cinema. I'm afraid of escalators and dolls' eyes. But there aren't any words for this fear. The words haven't been invented.

She said, 'I'll like it again when the rain stops.'

'You weren't liking it just now, were you? Down by the river.'

'Well,' she said, 'no. Not much.'

'It was a bit ghostly down there tonight. What can you expect? Never pick a place in fine weather.' (Or anything else either he thought.) 'There are too many pines about,' he said. 'They shut you in.'

'Yes.'

But it wasn't the black pines, she thought, or the sky without stars, or the thin hunted moon, or the lowering, flat-topped hills, or the tor and the big stones. It was the river.

'The river is very silent,' she'd said. 'Is that because it's so full?'

'One gets used to the noise, I suppose. Let's go in and light the bedroom fire. I wish we had a drink. I'd give a lot for a drink, wouldn't you?'

'We can have some coffee.'

As they walked back he'd kept his head turned towards the water.

'Curiously metallic it looks by this light. Not like water at all.'

'It looks smooth as if it were frozen. And much wider.'

'Frozen – no. Very alive in an uncanny way. Streaming hair,' he'd said as if he were talking to himself. So he'd felt it too. She lay remembering how the brown broken-surfaced, fast-running river had changed by moonlight. Things are more powerful than people. I've always believed that. (You're not my daughter if you're afraid of a horse. You're not my daughter if you're afraid of being seasick. You're not my daughter if you're afraid of the shape of a hill, or the moon when it is growing old. In fact you're not my daughter.)

'It isn't silent now is it?' she said. 'The river I mean.'

'No, it makes a row from up here.' He yawned. 'I'll put another log on the fire. It was very kind of Ransom to let us have that coal and wood. He didn't promise any luxuries of that sort when we took the cottage. He's not a bad chap, is he?'

'He's got a heart. And he must be wise to the climate after all.'

'Well I like it,' he said as he got back into bed, 'in spite of the rain. Let's be happy here.'

'Yes, let's.'

That's the second time. He said that before. He'd said it the first day they came. Then too she hadn't answered 'yes let's' at once because fear which had been waiting for her had come up to her and touched her, and it had been several seconds before she could speak.

'That must have been an otter we saw this evening,' he said, 'much too big for a water rat. I'll tell Ransom. He'll be very excited.'

'Why?'

'Oh, they're rather rare in these parts.'

'Poor devils, I bet they have an awful time if they're rare. What'll he do? Organize a hunt? Perhaps he won't, we've agreed that he's soft-hearted. This is a bird sanctuary, did you know? It's all sorts of things. I'll tell him about that yellow-breasted one. Maybe he'll know what it was.'

That morning she had watched it fluttering up and down the

window pane – a flash of yellow in the rain. 'Oh what a pretty bird.' Fear is yellow. You're yellow. She's got a broad streak of yellow. They're quite right, fear is yellow. 'Isn't it pretty? And isn't it persistent? It's determined to get in. . . .'

'I'm going to put this light out,' he said. 'It's no use. The fire's better.'

He struck a match to light another cigarette and when it flared she saw the deep hollows under his eyes, the skin stretched taut over his cheekbones, and the thin bridge of his nose. He was smiling as if he knew what she'd been thinking.

'Is there anything you're not afraid of in these moods of yours?'

'You,' she said. The match went out. Whatever happened, she thought. Whatever you did. Whatever I did. Never you. D'you hear me?

'Good.' He laughed. 'That's a relief.'

'Tomorrow will be fine, you'll see. We'll be lucky.'

'Don't depend on our luck. You ought to know better by this time,' he muttered. 'But you're the sort who never knows better. Unfortunately we're both the sort who never know better.'

'Are you tired? You sound tired.'

'Yes.' He sighed and turned away. 'I am rather.' When she said, 'I must put the light on, I want some aspirin,' he didn't answer, and she stretched her arm over him and touched the switch of the dim electric bulb. He was sleeping. The lighted cigarette had fallen on to the sheet.

'Good thing I saw that,' she said aloud. She put the cigarette out and threw it through the window, found the aspirin, emptied the ashtray, postponing the moment when she must lie down stretched out straight, listening, when she'd shut her eyes only to feel them click open again.

'Don't go to sleep,' she thought lying there. 'Stay awake and comfort me. I'm frightened. There's something here to be frightened of, I tell you. Why can't you feel it? When you said, let's be happy, that first day, there was a tap dripping somewhere into a full basin, playing a gay and horrible tune. Didn't you hear it? I heard it. Don't turn away and sigh and sleep. Stay awake and comfort me.'

Nobody's going to comfort you, she told herself, you ought to know better. Pull yourself together. There was a time when you weren't afraid. Was there? When? When was that time? Of course there was. Go on. Pull yourself together, pull yourself to pieces. There was a time. There was a time. Besides I'll sleep soon. There's always sleeping, and it'll be fine tomorrow.

'I knew it would be fine today,' she thought when she saw the sunlight through the flimsy curtains. 'The first fine day we've had.'

'Are you awake,' she said. 'It's a fine day. I had such a funny dream,' she said, still staring at the sunlight. 'I dreamt I was walking in a wood and the trees were groaning and then I dreamt of the wind in telegraph wires, well a bit like that, only very loud. I can still hear it – really I swear I'm not making this up. It's still in my head and it isn't like anything else except a bit like the wind in telegraph wires.'

'It's a lovely day,' she said and touched his hand.

'My dear, you are cold. I'll get a hot water bottle and some tea. I'll get it because I'm feeling very energetic this morning, you stay still for once!'

'Why don't you answer,' she said sitting up and peering at him. 'You're frightening me,' she said, her voice rising. 'You're frightening me. Wake up,' she said and shook him. As soon as she touched him her heart swelled till it reached her throat. It swelled and grew jagged claws and the claws clutched her driving in deep. 'Oh God,' she said and got up and drew the curtains and saw his face in the sun. 'Oh God,' she said staring at his face in the sun and knelt by the bed with his hand in her two hands not speaking not thinking any longer.

The doctor said, 'You didn't hear anything during the night?'

'I thought it was a dream.'

'Oh! You thought it was a dream. I see. What time did you wake up?'

'I don't know. We kept the clock in the other room because it had a loud tick. About half past eight or nine, I suppose.'

'You knew what had happened of course.'

'I wasn't sure. At first I wasn't sure.'

'But what did you do? It was past ten when you telephoned. What did you do?'

Not a word of comfort. Suspicious. He has small eyes and bushy eyebrows and he looks suspicious.

She said, 'I put on a coat and went to Mr Ransom's, where there's a telephone. I ran all the way but it seemed a long way.'

'But that oughtn't to have taken you more than ten minutes at most.'

'No, but it seemed very long. I ran but I didn't seem to be moving. When I got there everybody was out and the room where the telephone is was locked. The front door is always open but he locks that room when he goes out. I went back into the road but there was no one there. Nobody in the house and nobody in the road and nobody on the slope of the hill. There were a lot of sheets and men's shirts hanging on a line waving. And the sun of course. It was our first day. The first fine day we've had.'

She looked at the doctor's face, stopped, and went on in a different voice.

'I walked up and down for a bit. I didn't know what to do.

Then I thought I might be able to break the door in. So I tried and I did. A board broke and I got in. But it seemed a long time before anybody answered.'

She thought, Yes, of course I knew. I was late because I had to stay there listening. I heard it then. It got louder and closer and it was in the room with me. I heard the sound of the river.

I heard the sound of the river.

THE LEFT BANK

Preface to a Selection of Stories from The Left Bank

The Left Bank, *with the sub-title 'sketches and studies of present-day Bohemian Paris', was first published by Jonathan Cape in 1927. It was Jean Rhys's first book, a collection of twenty-two stories with a long Preface by Ford Madox Ford whose recognition and encouragement of her talent had brought the book into being. Miss Rhys now feels that many of the sketches do not merit republication, but she has approved the following selection made by her publisher.*

The greater part of Ford Madox Ford's Preface consisted of his own portrait of the Left Bank and his thoughts about its significance. It ends, however, with some pages on Jean Rhys's work, and these still remain appropriate to her writing as a whole, as well as interesting in showing the impression her artistry made on the appearance of its first signs.

. . . What – what in heaven's name? – is the lot of the opposition who must wait till their Thought is the accepted Thought of tomorrow?

To some extent the answer will be found in Miss Rhys's book for which I have not so much been asked, as I have asked to be allowed the privilege of supplying this Preface. Setting aside for a moment the matter of her very remarkable technical gifts, I should like to call attention to her profound knowledge of the life of the Left Bank – of many of the Left Banks of the world. For something mournful – and certainly hard up! – attaches to almost all uses of the word *left*. The left hand has not the cunning of the right: and every city has its left bank. London has, round Bloomsbury, New York has, about Greenwich Village, so has Vienna – but Vienna is a little ruined everywhere since the glory of Austria, to the discredit of European civilization, has departed! Miss Rhys does not, I believe, know Greenwich Village, but so many of its products are to be found on the Left Bank of Paris that she may be said to know its products. And coming from the Antilles, with a terrifying insight and a terrific – an almost lurid! – passion for stating the case of the underdog, she has let her pen loose on the Left Banks of the Old World – on its gaols, its studios, its salons, its cafés, its criminals, its midinettes – with a bias of admiration for its midinettes and of sympathy for its lawbreakers. It is a note, a sympathy, of which we do not have too much in Occidental literature with its perennial bias towards satisfaction with things as they are. But it is a note which needs sounding, since the real activities of the world are seldom carried much forward by the accepted, or even by the Hautes Bourgeoisies!

When I, lately, edited a periodical, Miss Rhys sent in several communications with which I was immensely struck, and of which I published as many as I could. What struck me on the technical side – which does not much interest the Anglo-Saxon reader, but which is almost the only thing that interests me – was the singular instinct for form possessed by this young lady, an instinct for form being possessed by singularly few writers of English and by almost no English women writers. I say 'instinct', for that is what it appears to me to be: these sketches begin exactly where they should and end exactly when their job is done. No doubt the almost exclusive reading of French writers of a recent, but not the most recent, date has helped. For French youth of today, rejecting with violence and in a mystified state of soul, all that was French of yesterday, has rejected neatness of form as it eschews the austere or the benignant agnosticisms of Anatole France, or Renan and of all the High Bourgeoisie that eleven years ago today stood exclusively for France. The youth of France today is constructive, uncertain, rule of thumb, believing, passionate, and, aware that it works in a mist, it is determined violently not to be coldly critical, or critical at all.

Amongst the things that French youth rejects more violently than others is the descriptive passage, the getting of what, in my hot youth, used to be called atmosphere. I tried – for I am for ever meddling with the young! – very hard to induce the author of *The Left Bank* to introduce some sort of topography of that region, bit by bit, into her sketches – in the cunning way in which it would have been done by Flaubert or Maupassant, or by Mr Conrad 'getting in' the East in innumerable short stories from *Almayer* to *Rescue* . . . But would she do it? No! With cold deliberation, once her attention was called to the matter, she eliminated even such two or three words of descriptive matter as had crept into her work. Her business was with passion, hardship, emotions: the locality in which these things are endured is immaterial. So she hands you the Antilles with its sea and sky – 'the loveliest, deepest sea in the world – the Caribbean!' – the effects of landscape on the emotions and passions of a child being so penetrative, but lets Montparnasse, or London, or Vienna go. She is probably right. Something human should, indeed, be dearer to one than all the topographies of the world. . . .

. . . One likes, in short, to be connected with something good, and Miss Rhys's work seems to me to be so very good, so vivid, so extraordinarily distinguished by the rendering of passion, and so true, that I wish to be connected with it. I hope I shall bring her a few readers and so when – hundreds of years hence! – her ashes are translated to the Panthéon, in the voluminous pall, the cords of which are held by the most prominent of the Haute Bourgeoisie of France, a grain or so of my scattered and forgotten dust may go in too, in the folds.

FORD MADOX FORD

Illusion

I

Miss Bruce was quite an old inhabitant of the Quarter. For seven years she had lived there, in a little studio up five flights of stairs. She had painted portraits, exhibited occasionally at the Salon. She had even sold a picture sometimes – a remarkable achievement for Montparnasse, but possible, for I believe she was just clever enough and not too clever, though I am no judge of these matters.

She was a tall, thin woman, with large bones and hands and feet. One thought of her as a shining example of what character and training – British character and training – can do. After seven years in Paris she appeared utterly untouched, utterly unaffected, by anything hectic, slightly exotic or unwholesome. Going on all the time all round her were the cult of beauty and the worship of physical love: she just looked at her surroundings in her healthy, sensible way, and then dismissed them from her thoughts . . . rather like some sturdy rock with impotent blue waves washing round it.

When pretty women passed her in the streets or sat near her in restaurants she would look appraisingly with the artist's eye, and make a suitably critical remark. She exhibited no tinge of curiosity or envy. As for the others, the petites femmes, anxiously consulting the mirrors of their bags, anxiously and searchingly looking round with darkened eyelids: 'Those unfortunate people!' would say Miss Bruce. Not in a hard way, but broadmindedly, breezily: indeed with a thoroughly gentlemanly intonation. . . . Those unfortunate little people!

She always wore a neat serge dress in the summer and a neat tweed costume in the winter, brown shoes with low heels and cotton stockings. When she was going to parties she put on a black gown of crêpe de chine, just well enough cut, not extravagantly pretty.

In fact Miss Bruce was an exceedingly nice woman.

She powdered her nose as a concession to Paris; the rest of her face shone, beautifully washed, in the sunlight or the electric light as the case might be, with here and there a few rather lovable freckles.

She had, of course, like most of the English and American artists in Paris, a private income – a respectably large one, I believe. She knew most people and was intimate with nobody. We had been dining and lunching together, now and then, for two years, yet I only knew the outside of Miss Bruce – the cool, sensible, tidy English outside.

Well, we had an appointment on a hot, sunny afternoon, and I arrived to see her about three o'clock. I was met by a very perturbed concierge.

Mademoiselle had been in bed just one day, and, suddenly, last night about eight o'clock the pain had become terrible. The femme de ménage, 'Mame' Pichon who had stayed all day and she, the concierge, had consulted anxiously, had fetched a doctor and, at his recommendation, had had her conveyed to the English Hospital in an ambulance.

'She took nothing with her,' said the femme de ménage,

a thin and voluble woman. 'Nothing at all, pauvre Mademoiselle.' If Madame – that was me – would give herself the trouble to come up to the studio, here were the keys. I followed Madame Pichon up the stairs. I must go at once to Miss Bruce and take her some things. She must at least have nightgowns and a comb and brush.

'The keys of the wardrobe of Mademoiselle,' said Madame Pichon insinuatingly, and with rather a queer sidelong look at me, 'are in this small drawer. Ah, les voilà!'

I thanked her with a dismissing manner. Madame Pichon was not a favourite of mine, and with firmness I watched her walk slowly to the door, try to start a conversation, and then, very reluctantly, disappear. Then I turned to the wardrobe – a big, square, solid piece of old, dark furniture, suited for the square and solid coats and skirts of Miss Bruce. Indeed, most of her furniture was big and square. Some strain in her made her value solidity and worth more than grace or fantasies. It was difficult to turn the large key, but I managed it at last.

'Good Lord!' I remarked out loud. Then, being very much surprised I sat down on a chair and said: 'Well, what a funny girl!'

For Miss Bruce's wardrobe when one opened it was a glow of colour, a riot of soft silks . . . everything that one did not expect.

In the middle, hanging in the place of honour, was an evening dress of a very beautiful shade of old gold: near it another of flame colour: of two black dresses the one was touched with silver, the other with a jaunty embroidery of emerald and blue. There were a black and white check with a jaunty belt, a flowered crêpe de chine – positively flowered! – then a carnival costume complete with mask, then a huddle, a positive huddle of all colours, of all stuffs.

For one instant I thought of kleptomania, and dismissed

the idea. Dresses for models, then? Absurd! Who would spend thousands of francs on dresses for models. . . . No nightgowns here, in any case.

As I looked, hesitating, I saw in the corner a box without a lid. It contained a neat little range of smaller boxes: Rouge Fascination; Rouge Mandarine; Rouge Andalouse; several powders; kohl for the eyelids and paint for the eyelashes – an outfit for a budding Manon Lescaut. Nothing was missing: there were scents too.

I shut the door hastily. I had no business to look or to guess. But I guessed. I knew. Whilst I opened the other half of the wardrobe and searched the shelves for nightgowns I knew it all: Miss Bruce, passing by a shop, with the perpetual hunger to be beautiful and that thirst to be loved which is the real curse of Eve, well hidden under her neat dress, more or less stifled, more or less unrecognized.

Miss Bruce had seen a dress and had suddenly thought: in that dress perhaps. . . . And, immediately afterwards: why not? And had entered the shop, and, blushing slightly, had asked the price. That had been the first time: an accident, an impulse.

The dress must have been disappointing, yet beautiful enough, becoming enough to lure her on. Then must have begun the search for *the* dress, the perfect Dress, beautiful, beautifying, possible to be worn. And lastly, the search for illusion – a craving, almost a vice, the stolen waters and the bread eaten in secret of Miss Bruce's life.

Wonderful moment! When the new dress would arrive and would emerge smiling and graceful from its tissue paper.

'Wear me, give me life,' it would seem to say to her, 'and I will do my damnedest for you!' And, first, not unskilfully, for was she not a portrait painter? Miss Bruce would put on the powder, the Rouge Fascination, the rouge for the lips, lastly the dress – and she would gaze into the glass at a transformed self. She would sleep that night with a warm glow at her heart. No impossible thing, beauty and all that beauty brings. There close at hand, to be clutched if one dared. Somehow she never dared, next morning.

I thankfully seized a pile of nightgowns and sat down, rather miserably undecided. I knew she would hate me to have seen those dresses: 'Mame' Pichon would tell her that I had been to the armoire. But she must have her nightgowns. I went to lock the wardrobe doors and felt a sudden, irrational pity for the beautiful things inside. I imagined them, shrugging their silken shoulders, rustling, whispering about the *anglaise* who had dared to buy them in order to condemn them to life in the dark. . . . And I opened the door again.

The yellow dress appeared malevolent, slouching on its hanger; the black ones were mournful, only the little chintz frock smiled gaily, waiting for the supple body and limbs that should breathe life into it.

When I was allowed to see Miss Bruce a week afterwards I found her lying, clean, calm and sensible in the big ward – an appendicitis patient. They patched her up and two or three weeks later we dined together at our restaurant. At the coffee stage she said suddenly: 'I suppose you noticed my collection of frocks. Why should I not collect frocks? They fascinate me. The colour and all that. Exquisite sometimes!'

'Of course,' she added, carefully staring over my head at what appeared to me to be a very bad picture, 'I should never make such a fool of myself as to wear them. . . . They ought to be worn, I suppose.'

A plump, dark girl, near us, gazed into the eyes of her dark, plump escort, and lit a cigarette with the slightly affected movements of the non-smoker.

'Not bad hands and arms, that girl,' said Miss Bruce in her gentlemanly manner.

From a French Prison

THE old man and the little boy were the last of the queue of people waiting to show their permits and to be admitted to the parloir – a row of little boxes where on certain days prisoners may speak to their friends through a grating for a quarter of an hour.

The old man elbowed his way weakly, but with persistence, to the front, and when the warder shouted at him brutally to go back to his place he still advanced.

The warder yelled: 'Go back, I tell you. Don't you understand me? You are not French?' The old man shook his head. 'One sees that,' the warder said sarcastically. He gave him a push and the old man, puzzled, backed a few steps and leaned against the wall, waiting.

He had gentle, regular features, and a grey cropped moustache. He was miserably clothed, hatless, with a red scarf knotted round his neck. His eyes were clouded with a white film, the film one sees over the eyes of those threatened with blindness.

The little boy was very little; his arms and legs match-like. He held tightly on to the old man's hand and looked up at the warder with enormous brown eyes. There were several children in the queue.

One woman had brought two – a baby in her arms and another hanging on to her skirt. All the crowd was silent and overawed. The women stood with bent heads, glancing furtively at each other, not with the antagonism usual in women, but as if at companions.

From the foot of the staircase leading down from the room in which they waited, ran a very long whitewashed corridor, incredibly grim, and dark in spite of the whitewash. Here and there a warder sat close against the wall looking in its shadow like a huge spider – a bloated, hairy insect born of the darkness and of the dank smell.

There were very few men waiting, and nearly all the women were of the sort that trouble has whipped into a becoming meekness, but two girls near the staircase were painted and dressed smartly in bright colours. They laughed and talked, their eyes dark and defiant. One of them muttered: 'Sale flic, va' – as who should say: 'Let him be, you dirty cop!' when the warder had pushed the old man.

The queue looked frightened but pleased: an old woman like a rat huddled against the wall and chuckled. The warder balanced himself backwards and forwards from heel to toe, important and full of authority, like some petty god. There he was, the representative of honesty, of the law, of the stern forces of Good that punishes Evil. His forehead was low and barred by a perpetual frown, his jaw was heavy and protruding. A tall man, well set up. He looked with interest at the girl who had spoken, twirled his moustache and stuck his chest out. The queue waited patiently.

The parloir was like a row of telephone boxes without tops.

Along the platform overhead one saw the legs of yet another warder, marching backwards and forwards, listening to the conversations beneath him. The voices all sounded on one note – a monotonous and never-ending buzz.

The first warder looked at his watch and began to fling all the doors open with ferocious bangs. A stream of rather startled-looking people poured out, their visits over. He beckoned to the queue for others to come forward and take their places. He called the dark-eyed girl who had spoken, staring hard at her as she passed, but she was busy, looking into her mirror, powdering her face, preparing for her interview.

To the opposite door of each box came a prisoner, gripping on to the bars, straining forward to see his visitor and starting at every sound. For the quarter of an hour would seem terribly short to him and always he listened for the shout of the warder to summon him away and always he feared not being on the alert to answer it.

The monotonous buzz of conversation began again. The warder on the roof sighed and then yawned; the warder outside twirled his moustache and stared at the wall. Then a fresh stream with permits came up the stairs and he tramped forward weightily to marshal them into line.

When the quarter of an hour was over the doors were flung open again.

As the dark-eyed girl passed out the warder stared hard at her and she stared back, not giving an inch, defiant and provocative. He half smiled and actually drew back to let her pass.

The old man came last, shuffling along, more bewildered than ever. At the gate of the prison all the permits must be given up, but he trailed out unheeding. The important person who was taking those documents shouted: 'Hé! your permit!' and added: 'Monsieur,' with cynicism. The old man looked frightened, his eyes filled with tears, and when his permit was snatched from him he burst into a flood of words, waving his arms.

A woman stopped to explain to him that if he asked for it next visiting day it would be given back to him, but he did not understand.

'Allons. Allons,' said the warder at the gate authoritatively. 'Get along. Get along.'

Outside the people hurried to catch the tram back to Paris.

The two girls stepped out jauntily, with animated gestures and voices, but the old man walked sadly, his head bent, muttering to himself. By his side the little boy took tiny little trotting steps – three to the old man's one. His mouth drooped, his huge brown eyes stared solemnly at an incomprehensible world.

Mannequin

TWELVE o'clock. Déjeuner chez Jeanne Veron, Place Vendôme.

Anna, dressed in the black cotton, chemise-like garment of the mannequin off duty was trying to find her way along dark passages and down complicated flights of stairs to the underground room where lunch was served.

She was shivering, for she had forgotten her coat, and the garment that she wore was very short, sleeveless, displaying her rose-coloured stockings to the knee. Her hair was flamingly and honestly red; her eyes, which were very gentle in expression, brown and heavily shadowed with kohl; her face small and pale under its professional rouge. She was fragile, like a delicate child, her arms pathetically thin. It was to her legs that she owed this dazzling, this incredible opportunity.

Madame Veron, white-haired with black eyes, incredibly distinguished, who had given them one sweeping glance, the glance of the connoisseur, smiled imperiously and engaged her at an exceedingly small salary. As a beginner, Madame explained, Anna could not expect more. She was to wear the jeune fille dresses. Another smile, another sharp glance.

Anna was conducted from the Presence by an underling who

helped her to take off the frock she had worn temporarily for the interview. Aspirants for an engagement are always dressed in a model of the house.

She had spent yesterday afternoon in a delirium tempered by a feeling of exaggerated reality, and in buying the necessary make up. It had been such a forlorn hope, answering the advertisement.

The morning had been dreamlike. At the back of the wonderfully decorated salons she had found an unexpected sombreness; the place, empty, would have been dingy and melancholy, countless puzzling corridors and staircases, a rabbit warren and a labyrinth. She despaired of ever finding her way.

In the mannequins' dressing-room she spent a shy hour making up her face – in an extraordinary and distinctive atmosphere of slimness and beauty; white arms and faces vivid with rouge; raucous voices and the smell of cosmetics; silken lingerie. Coldly critical glances were bestowed upon Anna's reflection in the glass. None of them looked at her directly. . . . A depressing room, taken by itself, bare and cold, a very inadequate conservatory for these human flowers. Saleswomen in black rushed in and out, talking in sharp voices; a very old woman hovered, helpful and shapeless, showing Anna where to hang her clothes, presenting to her the black garment that Anna was wearing, going to lunch. She smiled with professional motherliness, her little, sharp, black eyes travelling rapidly from la nouvelle's hair to her ankles and back again.

She was Madame Pecard, the dresser.

Before Anna had spoken a word she was called away by a small boy in buttons to her destination in one of the salons: there, under the eye of a vendeuse, she had to learn the way to wear the innocent and springlike air and garb of the jeune fille. Behind a yellow, silken screen she was hustled into a leather coat and paraded under the cold eyes of an American buyer.

This was the week when the spring models are shown to important people from big shops all over Europe and America: the most critical week of the season. . . . The American buyer said that he would have that, but with an inch on to the collar and larger cuffs. In vain the saleswoman, in her best English with its odd Chicago accent, protested that that would completely ruin the chic of the model. The American buyer knew what he wanted and saw that he got it.

The vendeuse sighed, but there was a note of admiration in her voice. She respected Americans: they were not like the English, who, under a surface of annoying moroseness of manner, were notoriously timid and easy to turn round your finger.

'Was that all right?' Behind the screen one of the saleswomen smiled encouragingly and nodded. The other shrugged her shoulders. She had small, close-set eyes, a long thin nose and tight lips of the regulation puce colour. Behind her silken screen Anna sat on a high white stool. She felt that she appeared charming and troubled. The white and gold of the salon suited her red hair.

A short morning. For the mannequin's day begins at ten and the process of making up lasts an hour. The friendly saleswoman volunteered the information that her name was Jeannine, that she was in the lingerie, that she considered Anna rudement jolie, that noon was Anna's lunch hour. She must go down the corridor and up those stairs, through the big salon then. . . . Anyone would tell her. But Anna, lost in the labyrinth, was too shy to ask her way. Besides, she was not sorry to have time to brace herself for the ordeal. She had reached the regions of utility and oilcloth: the decorative salons were far overhead. Then the smell of food – almost visible, it was so cloudlike and heavy – came to her nostrils, and high-noted, and sibilant, a buzz of conversation made her draw a deep breath. She pushed a door open.

She was in a big, very low-ceilinged room, all the floor space occupied by long wooden tables with no cloths. . . . She was sitting at the mannequins' table, gazing at a thick and hideous white china plate, a twisted tin fork, a wooden-handled stained knife, a tumbler so thick it seemed unbreakable.

There were twelve mannequins at Jeanne Veron's: six of them were lunching, the others still paraded, goddess-like, till their turn came for rest and refreshment. Each of the twelve was of a distinct and separate type: each of the twelve knew her type and kept to it, practising rigidly in clothing, manner, voice and conversation.

Round the austere table were now seated: Babette, the gamine, the traditional blonde enfant: Mona, tall and darkly beautiful, the femme fatale, the wearer of sumptuous evening gowns. Georgette was the garçonne: Simone with green eyes Anna knew instantly for a cat whom men would and did adore, a sleek, white, purring, long-lashed creature. . . . Eliane was the star of the collection.

Eliane was frankly ugly and it did not matter: no doubt Lilith, from whom she was obviously descended, had been ugly too. Her hair was henna-tinted, her eyes small and black, her complexion bad under her thick make-up. Her hips were extraordinarily slim, her hands and feet exquisite, every movement she made was as graceful as a flower's in the wind. Her walk . . . But it was her walk which made her the star there and earned her a salary quite fabulous for Madame Veron's, where large salaries were not the rule. . . . Her walk and her 'chic of the devil' which lit an expression of admiration in even the cold eyes of American buyers.

Eliane was a quiet girl, pleasant-mannered. She wore a ring with a beautiful emerald on one long, slim finger, and in her small eyes were both intelligence and mystery.

Madame Pecard, the dresser, was seated at the head of the

mannequin's table, talking loudly, unlistened to, and gazing benevolently at her flock.

At other tables sat the sewing girls, pale-faced, black-frocked – the workers, heroically gay, but with the stamp of labour on them: and the saleswomen. The mannequins, with their sensual, blatant charms and their painted faces were watched covertly, envied and apart.

Babette the blonde enfant was next to Anna, and having started the conversation with a few good, round oaths at the quality of the sardines, announced proudly that she could speak English and knew London very well. She began to tell Anna the history of her adventures in the city of coldness, dark and fogs. . . . She had gone to a job as a mannequin in Bond Street and the villainous proprietor of the shop having tried to make love to her and she being rigidly virtuous, she had left. And another job, Anna must figure to herself, had been impossible to get, for she, Babette, was too small and slim for the Anglo-Saxon idea of a mannequin.

She stopped to shout in a loud voice to the woman who was serving: 'Hé, my old one, don't forget your little Babette. . . .'

Opposite, Simone the cat and the sportive Georgette were having a low-voiced conversation about the triste-ness of a monsieur of their acquaintance. 'I said to him,' Georgette finished decisively, 'Nothing to be done, my rabbit. You have not looked at me well, little one. In my place would you not have done the same?'

She broke off when she realized that the others were listening, and smiled in a friendly way at Anna.

She too, it appeared, had ambitions to go to London because the salaries were so much better there. Was it difficult? Did they really like French girls? Parisiennes?

The conversation became general.

'The English boys are nice,' said Babette, winking one

divinely candid eye. 'I had a chic type who used to take me to dinner at the Empire Palace. Oh, a pretty boy. . . .'

'It is the most chic restaurant in London,' she added importantly.

The meal reached the stage of dessert. The other tables were gradually emptying; the mannequins all ordered very strong coffee, several a liqueur. Only Mona and Eliane remained silent; Eliane, because she was thinking of something else; Mona, because it was her type, her genre to be haughty.

Her hair swept away from her white, narrow forehead and her small ears: her long earrings nearly touching her shoulders, she sipped her coffee with a disdainful air. Only once, when the blonde enfant, having engaged in a passage of arms with the waitress and got the worst of it was momentarily discomfited and silent, Mona narrowed her eyes and smiled an astonishingly cruel smile.

As soon as her coffee was drunk she got up and went out.

Anna produced a cigarette, and Georgette, perceiving instantly that here was the sportive touch, her genre, asked for one and lit it with a devil-may-care air. Anna eagerly passed her cigarettes round, but the Mère Pecard interfered weightily. It was against the rules of the house for the mannequins to smoke, she wheezed. The girls all lit their cigarettes and smoked. The Mère Pecard rumbled on: 'A caprice, my children. All the world knows that mannequins are capricious. Is it not so?' She appealed to the rest of the room.

As they went out Babette put her arm round Anna's waist and whispered: 'Don't answer Madame Pecard. We don't like her. We never talk to her. She spies on us. She is a camel.'

That afternoon Anna stood for an hour to have a dress draped on her. She showed this dress to a stout Dutch lady buying for the Hague, to a beautiful South American with pearls, to a silver-haired American gentleman who wanted an evening cape for his daughter of seventeen, and to a hook-nosed, odd English lady of title who had a loud voice and dressed, under her furs, in a grey jersey and stout boots.

The American gentleman approved of Anna, and said so, and Anna gave him a passionately grateful glance. For, if the vendeuse Jeannine had been uniformly kind and encouraging, the other, Madame Tienne, had been as uniformly disapproving and had once even pinched her arm hard.

About five o'clock Anna became exhausted. The four white and gold walls seemed to close in on her. She sat on her high white stool staring at a marvellous nightgown and fighting an intense desire to rush away. Anywhere! Just to dress and rush away anywhere, from the raking eyes of the customers and the pinching fingers of Irene.

'I will one day. I can't stick it,' she said to herself. 'I won't be able to stick it.' She had an absurd wish to gasp for air.

Jeannine came and found her like that.

'It is hard at first, hein? . . . One asks oneself: Why? For what good? It is all idiot. We are all so. But we go on. Do not worry about Irene.' She whispered: 'Madame Veron likes you very much. I heard her say so.'

At six o'clock Anna was out in the rue de la Paix; her fatigue forgotten, the feeling that now she really belonged to the great, maddening city possessed her and she was happy in her beautifully cut tailor-made and a beret.

Georgette passed her and smiled; Babette was in a fur coat.

All up the street the mannequins were coming out of the shops, pausing on the pavements a moment, making them as gay and as beautiful as beds of flowers before they walked swiftly away and the Paris night swallowed them up.

Tea with an Artist

IT WAS obvious that this was not an Anglo-Saxon: he was too gay, too dirty, too unreserved and in his little eyes was such a mellow comprehension of all the sins and the delights of life. He was drinking rapidly one glass of beer after another, smoking a long, curved pipe, and beaming contentedly on the world. The woman with him wore a black coat and skirt; she had her back to us.

I said: 'Who's the happy man in the corner? I've never seen him before.'

My companion who knew everybody answered: 'That's Verhausen. As mad as a hatter.'

'Madder than most people here?' I asked.

'Oh, yes, really dotty. He has got a studio full of pictures that he will never show to anyone.'

I asked: 'What pictures? His own pictures?'

'Yes, his own pictures. They're damn good, they say.' . . . Verhausen had started out by being a Prix de Rome and he had had a big reputation in Holland and Germany, once upon a time. He was a Fleming. But the old fellow now refused to exhibit, and went nearly mad with anger if he were pressed to sell anything.

'A pose?'

My friend said: 'Well, I dunno. It's lasted a long time for a pose.'

He started to laugh.

'You know Van Hoyt. He knew Verhausen intimately in Antwerp, years ago. It seems he already hid his pictures up then. . . . He had evolved the idea that it was sacrilege to sell them. Then he married some young and flighty woman from Brussels, and she would not stand it. She nagged and nagged: she wanted lots of money and so on and so on. He did not listen even. So she gave up arguing and made arrangements with a Jew dealer from Amsterdam when he was not there. It is said that she broke into his studio and passed the pictures out of the window. Five of the best. Van Hoyt said that Verhausen cried like a baby when he knew. He simply sat and sobbed. Perhaps he also beat the lady. In any case she left him soon afterwards and eventually Verhausen turned up, here, in Montparnasse. The woman now with him he had picked up in some awful brothel in Antwerp. She must have been good to him, for he says now that the Fallen are the only women with souls. They will walk on the necks of all the others in Heaven . . .' And my friend concluded: 'A rum old bird. But a bit of a back number, now, of course.'

I said: 'It's a perverted form of miserliness, I suppose. I should like to see his pictures, or is that impossible? I like his face.'

My friend said carelessly: 'It's possible, I believe. He sometimes shows them to people. It's only that he will not exhibit and will not sell. I dare say Van Hoyt could fix it up.'

Verhausen's studio was in the real Latin Quarter which lies to the north of the Montparnasse district and is shabbier and not cosmopolitan yet. It was an ancient, narrow street of uneven houses, a dirty, beautiful street, full of mauve shadows. A policeman stood limply near the house, his expression that of contemplative stupefaction: a yellow dog lay stretched philosophically on the cobblestones of the roadway. The concierge said without interest that Monsieur Verhausen's studio was on the quatrième à droite. I toiled upwards.

I knocked three times. There was a subdued rustling within. . . . A fourth time: as loudly as I could. The door opened a little and Mr Verhausen's head appeared in the opening. I read suspicion in his eyes and I smiled as disarmingly as I could. I said something about Mr Van Hoyt – his own kind invitation, my great pleasure.

Verhausen continued to scrutinize me through huge spectacles: then he smiled with a sudden irradiation, stood away from the door and bowing deeply, invited me to enter. The room was big, all its walls encumbered on the floor with unframed canvases, all turned with their backs to the wall. It was very much cleaner than I had expected: quite clean and even dustless. On a table was spread a white cloth and there were blue cups and saucers and a plate of gingerbread cut into slices and thickly buttered. Mr Verhausen rubbed his hands and said with a pleased, childlike expression and in astonishingly good English that he had prepared an English tea that was quite ready because he had expected me sooner.

We sat on straight-backed chairs and sipped solemnly.

Mr Verhausen looked exactly as he had looked in the café, his blue eyes behind the spectacles at once naive and wise, his waistcoat spotted with reminiscences of many meals.

But a delightful personality – comfortable and comforting. His long, curved pipes hung in a row on the wall; they made the whole room look Dutchly homely. We discussed Montparnasse with gravity.

He said suddenly: 'Now you have drunk your second cup of

tea you shall see my pictures. Two cups of tea all English must have before they contemplate works of art.'

He had jumped up with a lightness surprising in a bulky man and with similar alacrity drew an easel near a window and proceeded to put pictures on it without any comment. They were successive outbursts of colour: it took me a little time to get used to them. I imagine that they were mostly, but not all, impressionist. But what fascinated me at first was his way of touching the canvases – his loving, careful hands.

After a time he seemed to forget that I was there and looked at them himself, anxiously and critically, his head on one side, frowning and muttering to himself in Flemish. A landscape pleased me here and there: they were mostly rough and brilliant. But the heads were very minutely painted and . . . Dutch! A woman stepping into a tub of water under a shaft of light had her skin turned to gold.

Then he produced a larger canvas, changed the position of the easel and turned to me with a little grunt. I said slowly: 'I think that is a great picture. Great art!'

. . . A girl seated on a sofa in a room with many mirrors held a glass of green liqueur. Dark-eyed, heavy-faced, with big, sturdy peasant's limbs, she was entirely destitute of lightness or grace.

But all the poisonous charm of the life beyond the pale was in her pose, and in her smouldering eyes – all its deadly bitterness and fatigue in her fixed smile.

He received my compliments with pleasure, but with the quite superficial pleasure of the artist who is supremely indifferent to the opinion that other people may have about his work. And, just as I was telling him that the picture reminded me of a portrait of Manet's, the original came in from outside, carrying a string bag full of greengroceries. Mr Verhausen started a little when he saw her and rubbed his hands again –

apologetically this time. He said: 'This, Madame, is my little Marthe. Mademoiselle Marthe Baesen.'

She greeted me with reserve and glanced at the picture on the easel with an inscrutable face. I said to her: 'I have been admiring Mr Verhausen's work.'

She said: 'Yes, Madame?' with the inflexion of a question and left the room with her string bag.

The old man said to me: 'Marthe speaks no English and French very badly. She is a true Fleming. Besides, she is not used to visitors.'

There was a feeling of antagonism in the studio now. Mr Verhausen fidgeted and sighed restlessly. I said, rather with hesitation: 'Mr Verhausen, is it true that you object to exhibiting and to selling your pictures?'

He looked at me over his spectacles, and the suspicious look, the look of an old Jew when counting his money, came again into his eyes.

'Object, Madame? I object to nothing. I am an artist. But I do not wish to sell my pictures. And, as I do not wish to sell them, exhibiting is useless. My pictures are precious to me. They are precious, most probably, to no one else.'

He chuckled and added with a glint of malice in his eyes: 'When I am dead Marthe will try to sell them and not succeed, probably. I am forgotten now. Then she will burn them. She dislikes rubbish, the good Marthe.'

Marthe re-entered the room as he said this. Her face was unpowdered but nearly unwrinkled, her eyes were clear with the shrewd, limited expression of the careful housewife – the look of small horizons and quick, hard judgments. Without the flame his genius had seen in her and had fixed for ever, she was heavy, placid and uninteresting – at any rate to me.

She said, in bad French: 'I have bought two artichokes

for . . .' I did not catch how many sous. He looked pleased and greedy.

In the street the yellow dog and the policeman had vanished. The café opposite the door had come alive and its gramophone informed the world that:

Souvent femme varie
Bien fol est qui s'y fie!

It was astonishing how the figure of the girl on the sofa stayed in my mind: it blended with the coming night, the scent of Paris and the hard blare of the gramophone. And I said to myself: 'Is it possible that all that charm, such as it was, is gone?'

And then I remembered the way in which she had touched his cheek with her big hands. There was in that movement knowledge, and a certain sureness: as it were the ghost of a time when her business in life had been the consoling of men.

Mixing Cocktails

THE house in the hills was very new and very ugly, long and narrow, of unpainted wood, perched oddly on high posts, I think as a protection from wood ants. There were six rooms with a verandah that ran the whole length of the house. . . . But when you went up there, there was always the same sensation of relief and coolness – in the ugly house with the beginnings of a rose garden, after an hour's journey by boat and another hour and a half on horse-back, climbing slowly up. . . .

On the verandah, upon a wooden table with four stout legs, stood an enormous brass telescope. With it you spied out the steamers passing: the French mail on its way to Guadeloupe, the Canadian, the Royal Mail, which should have been stately and was actually the shabbiest of the lot. . . . Or an exciting stranger!

At night one gazed through it at the stars and pretended to be interested. . . . 'That's Venus. . . . Oh, is that Venus. . . . And that's the Southern Cross. . . .' An unloaded shotgun leant up in one corner; there were always plenty of straw rockingchairs and a canvas hammock with many cushions.

From the verandah one looked down the green valley sloping to the sea, but from the other side of the house one could only see the mountains, lovely but melancholy as mountains always are to a child.

Lying in the hammock, swinging cautiously for the ropes creaked, one dreamt. . . . The morning dream was the best – very early, before the sun was properly up. The sea was then a very tender blue, like the dress of the Virgin Mary, and on it were little white triangles. The fishing boats.

A very short dream, the morning dream – mostly about what one would do with the endless blue day. One would bathe in the pool: perhaps one would find treasure. . . . Morgan's Treasure. For who does not know that, just before he was captured and I think hung at Kingston, Jamaica, Morgan buried his treasure in the Dominican mountains. . . . A wild place, Dominica. Savage and lost. Just the place for Morgan to hide his treasure in.

It was very difficult to look at the sea in the middle of the day. The light made it so flash and glitter: it was necessary to screw the eyes up tight before looking. Everything was still and languid, worshipping the sun.

The midday dream was languid too – vague, tinged with melancholy as one stared at the hard, blue, blue sky. It was sure to be interrupted by someone calling to one to come in out of the sun. One was not to sit in the sun. One had been told not to be in the sun. . . . One would one day regret freckles.

So the late afternoon was the best time on the verandah, but it was spoiled for all the rest were there. . . .

So soon does one learn the bitter lesson that humanity is never content just to differ from you and let it go at that. Never. They must interfere, actively and grimly, between your thoughts and yourself – with the passionate wish to level up everything and everybody.

I am speaking to you; do you not hear? You must break

yourself of your habit of never listening. You have such an absent-minded expression. Try not to look vague. . . .

So rude!

The English aunt gazes and exclaims at intervals: 'The colours. . . . How exquisite! . . . Extraordinary that so few people should visit the West Indies. . . . That *sea*. . . . Could anything be more lovely?'

It is a purple sea with a sky to match it. The Caribbean. The deepest, the loveliest in the world. . . .

Sleepily but tactfully, for she knows it delights my father, she admires the roses, the hibiscus, the humming birds. Then she starts to nod. She is always falling asleep, at the oddest moments. It is the unaccustomed heat.

I should like to laugh at her, but I am a well-behaved little girl. . . . Too well-behaved. . . . I long to be like Other People! The extraordinary, ungetatable, oddly cruel Other People, with their way of wantonly hurting and then accusing you of being thin-skinned, sulky, vindictive or ridiculous. All because a hurt and puzzled little girl has retired into her shell.

The afternoon dream is a materialistic one. . . . It is of the days when one shall be plump and beautiful instead of pale and thin: perfectly behaved instead of awkward. . . . When one will wear sweeping dresses and feathered hats and put gloves on with ease and delight. . . . And of course, of one's marriage: the dark moustache and perfectly creased trousers. . . . Vague, that.

The verandah gets dark very quickly. The sun sets: at once night and the fireflies.

A warm, velvety, sweet-smelling night, but frightening and disturbing if one is alone in the hammock. Ann Twist, our cook, the old obeah woman has told me: 'You all must'n look too much at de moon . . .'

If you fall asleep in the moonlight you are bewitched, it seems . . . the moon does bad things to you if it shines on you when you sleep. Repeated often . . .

So, shivering a little, I go into the room for the comfort of my father working out his chess problem from the *Times Weekly Edition*. Then comes my nightly duty of mixing cocktails.

In spite of my absentmindedness I mix cocktails very well and swizzle them better (our cocktails, in the West Indies, are drunk frothing, and the instrument with which one froths them is called a swizzle-stick) than anyone else in the house.

I measure out angostura and gin, feeling important and happy, with an uncanny intuition as to how strong I must make each separate drink.

Here then is something I can do. . . . Action, they say, is more worthy than dreaming. . . .

Again the Antilles

THE editor of the *Dominica Herald and Leeward Islands Gazette* lived in a tall, white house with green Venetian blinds which overlooked our garden. I used often to see him looking solemnly out of his windows and would gaze solemnly back, for I thought him a very awe-inspiring person.

He wore gold-rimmed spectacles and dark clothes always – not for him the frivolity of white linen even on the hottest day – a stout little man of a beautiful shade of coffee-colour, he was known throughout the Island as Papa Dom.

A born rebel, this editor: a firebrand. He hated the white people, not being quite white, and he despised the black ones, not being quite black. . . . 'Coloured' we West Indians call the intermediate shades, and I used to think that being coloured embittered him.

He was against the Government, against the English, against the Island's being a Crown Colony and the Town Board's new system of drainage. He was also against the Mob, against the gay and easy morality of the negroes and 'the horde of priests and nuns that overrun our unhappy Island', against the existence of the Anglican bishop and the Catholic bishop's new palace.

He wrote seething articles against that palace which was

then being built, partly by voluntary labour – until, one night his house was besieged by a large mob of the faithful, throwing stones and howling for his blood. He appeared on his verandah, frightened to death. In the next issue of his paper he wrote a long account of the 'riot': according to him it had been led by several well-known Magdalenes, then, as always, the most ardent supporters of Christianity.

After that, though, he let the Church severely alone, acknowledging that it was too strong for him.

I cannot imagine what started the quarrel between himself and Mr Hugh Musgrave.

Mr Hugh Musgrave I regarded as a dear, but peppery. Twenty years of the tropics and much indulgence in spices and cocktails does have that effect. He owned a big estate, just outside the town of Roseau, cultivated limes and sugar canes and employed a great deal of labour, but he was certainly neither ferocious nor tyrannical.

Suddenly, however, there was the feud in full swing.

There was in the *Dominica Herald and Leeward Islands Gazette* a column given up to letters from readers and, in this column, writing under the pseudonyms of Pro Patria, Indignant, Liberty and Uncle Tom's Cabin, Papa Dom let himself go. He said what he thought about Mr Musgrave and Mr Musgrave replied: briefly and sternly as befits an Englishman of the governing class. . . . Still he replied.

It was most undignified, but the whole Island was hugely delighted. Never had the *Herald* had such a sale.

Then Mr Musgrave committed, according to Papa Dom, some specially atrocious act of tyranny. Perhaps he put a fence up where he should not have, or overpaid an unpopular overseer or supported the wrong party on the Town Board. . . . At any rate Papa Dom wrote in the next issue of the paper this passionate and unforgettable letter:

'It is a saddening and a dismal sight,' it ended, 'to contemplate the degeneracy of a stock. How far is such a man removed from the ideals of true gentility, from the beautiful description of a contemporary, possibly, though not certainly, the Marquis of Montrose, left us by Shakespeare, the divine poet and genius.

'*He was a very gentle, perfect knight. . . .*'

Mr Musgrave took his opportunity:

'DEAR SIR,' he wrote,

'I never read your abominable paper. But my attention has been called to a scurrilous letter about myself which you published last week. The lines quoted were written, not by Shakespeare but by Chaucer, though you cannot of course be expected to know that, and run

He never yet no vilonye had sayde
In al his lyf, unto no manner of wight –
He was a verray parfit, gentil knyght.

'It is indeed a saddening and a dismal thing that the names of great Englishmen should be thus taken in vain by the ignorant of another race and colour.'

Mr Musgrave had really written 'damn niggers'.

Papa Dom was by no means crushed. Next week he replied with dignity as follows:

'My attention has been called to your characteristic letter. I accept your correction though I understand that in the mind of the best authorities there are grave doubts, very grave doubts indeed, as to the authorship of the lines, and indeed the other works of the immortal Swan of Avon. However, as I do not write with works of reference in front of me, as you most certainly do, I will not dispute the point.

'The conduct of an English gentleman who stoops to acts of tyranny and abuse cannot be described as gentle or perfect. I fail to see that it matters whether it is Shakespeare, Chaucer or the Marquis of Montrose who administers from down the ages the much-needed reminder and rebuke.'

I wonder if I shall ever again read the *Dominica Herald and Leeward Islands Gazette*.

Hunger

LAST night I took an enormous dose of valerian to make me sleep. I have awakened this morning very calm and rested, but with shaky hands.

It doesn't matter. I am not hungry either: that's a good thing as there is not the slightest prospect of my having anything to eat. I could of course buy a loaf, but we have been living on bread and nothing else for a long time. It gets monotonous. Also it's damned salt. . . .

Starvation – or rather semi-starvation – coffee in the morning, bread at midday, is exactly like everything else. It has its compensations, but they do not come at once. . . . To begin with it is a frankly awful business.

For the first twelve hours one is just astonished. No money: nothing to eat. . . . *Nothing!* . . . But that's farcical. There must be something one can do. Full of practical common sense you rush about; you search for the elusive 'something'. At night you have long dreams about food.

On the second day you have a bad headache. You feel pugnacious. You argue all day with an invisible and sceptical listener.

I tell you it is *not* my fault. . . . It happened suddenly, and

I have been ill. I had no time to make plans. *Can* you not see that one needs money to fight? Even with a hundred francs clear one could make plans.

I said *clear*. . . . A few hundred francs *clear*. There is the hotel to pay. Sell my clothes? . . . You cannot get any money for women's clothes in Paris. I tried for a place as a gouvernante yesterday. Of course I'm nervous and silly. So'd you be if . . .

Oh God! leave me alone. I don't care what you think; I don't.

On the third day one feels sick: on the fourth one starts crying very easily. . . . A bad habit that; it sticks.

On the fifth day. . . .

You awaken with a feeling of detachment; you are calm and godlike. It is to attain to that state that religious people fast.

Lying in bed, my arm over my eyes, I despise, utterly, my futile struggles of the last two years. What on earth have I been making such a fuss about? What does it matter, anyway? Women are always ridiculous when they struggle.

It is like being suspended over a precipice. You cling for dear life with people walking on your fingers. Women do not only walk: they stamp.

Primitive beings, most women.

But I have clung and made huge efforts to pull myself up. Three times I have . . . acquired resources. Means? Has she *means*? She has means. I have been a mannequin. I have been . . . no: not what you think. . . .

No good, any of it.

Well, you are doomed.

Once down you will never get up. *Did* anyone – did *any*body, I wonder, ever get up . . . once down?

Every few months there is bound to be a crisis. Every crisis will find you weaker.

If I were Russian I should long ago have accepted Fate: had I been French I should long ago have discovered and taken the back door out. I mean no disrespect to the French. They are logical. Had I been . . . SENSIBLE I should have hung on to being a mannequin with what it implies. As it is, I have struggled on, not cleverly. Almost against my own will. Don't I belong to the land of Lost Causes . . . England. . . .

If I had a glass of wine I would drink to that: the best of toasts:

To a Lost Cause: to All Lost Causes. . . .

Oh! the relief of letting go: tumbling comfortably into the abyss. . . .

Not such a terrible place after all. One day, no doubt, one will grow used to it. Lots of jolly people, here. . . .

No more effort.

Retrospection is a waste of the Fifth Day.

The best way is to spend it dreaming over some book like . . . *Dash* or . . . oh, *Dash*, again. . . .

Especially *Dash* number one. . . . There are words and sentences one can dream over for hours. . . .

Luckily we have both books: too torn to be worth selling.

I love her most before she has become too vicious.

It is as if your nerves were strung tight. Like violin strings. Anything: lovely words, or the sound of a concertina from the street: even a badly played piano can make one cry. Not with hunger or sadness. No!

But with the extraordinary beauty of life.

I have never gone without food for longer than five days, so I cannot amuse you any longer.

La Grosse Fifi

'THE sea,' said Mark Olsen, 'is exactly the colour of Reckett's blue this morning.'

Roseau turned her head to consider the smooth Mediterranean.

'I like it like that,' she announced, 'and I wish you wouldn't walk so fast. I loathe tearing along, and this road wasn't made to tear along anyhow.'

'Sorry,' said Mark, 'just a bad habit.'

They walked in silence, Mark thinking that this girl was a funny one, but he'd rather like to see a bit more of her. A pity Peggy seemed to dislike her – women were rather a bore with their likes and dislikes.

'Here's my hotel,' said the funny one. 'Doesn't it look awful?'

'You know,' Mark told her seriously, 'you really oughtn't to stay here. It's a dreadful place. Our patronne says that it's got a vile reputation – someone got stabbed or something, and the patron went to jail.'

'You don't say!' mocked Roseau.

'I do say. There's a room going at the pension.'

'Hate pensions.'

'Well, move then, move to St Paul or Juan les Pins – Peggy was saying yesterday. . . .'

'Oh Lord!' said Roseau rather impatiently, 'my hotel's all right. I'll move when I'm ready, when I've finished some work I'm doing. I think I'll go back to Paris – I'm getting tired of the Riviera, it's too tidy. Will you come in and have an aperitif?'

Her tone was so indifferent that Mark, piqued, accepted the invitation though the restaurant of that hotel really depressed him. It was so dark, so gloomy, so full of odd-looking, very odd-looking French people with abnormally loud voices even for French people. A faint odour of garlic floated in the air.

'Have a Deloso,' said Roseau. 'It tastes of anis,' she explained, seeing that he looked blank. 'It's got a kick in it.'

'Thank you,' said Mark. He put his sketches carefully on the table, then looking over Roseau's head his eyes became astonished and fixed. He said: 'Oh my Lord! What's that?'

'That's Fifi,' answered Roseau in a low voice and relaxing into a smile for the first time.

'Fifi! Of course – it would be – Good Lord! – Fifi!' His voice was awed. 'She's – she's terrific, isn't she?'

'She's a dear,' said Roseau unexpectedly.

Fifi was not terrific except metaphorically, but she was stout, well corseted – her stomach carefully arranged to form part of her chest. Her hat was large and worn with a rakish sideways slant, her rouge shrieked, and the lids of her protruding eyes were painted bright blue. She wore very long silver earrings; nevertheless her face looked huge – vast, and her voice was hoarse though there was nothing but Vichy water in her glass.

Her small, plump hands were covered with rings, her small, plump feet encased in very high-heeled, patent leather shoes.

Fifi was obvious in fact – no mistaking her mission in life. With her was a young man of about twenty-four. He would have been a handsome young man had he not plastered his face with white powder and worn his hair in a high mass above his forehead.

'She reminds me,' said Mark in a whisper, 'of Max Beerbohm's picture of the naughty lady considering Edward VII's head on a coin – You know, the "Ah! well, he'll always be Tum-Tum to me" one.'

'Yes,' said Roseau, 'she is Edwardian, isn't she?' For some unexplainable reason she disliked these jeers at Fifi, resented them even more than she resented most jeers. After all the lady looked so good-natured, such a good sort, her laugh was so jolly.

She said: 'Haven't you noticed what lots there are down here? Edwardian ladies, I mean – Swarms in Nice, shoals in Monte Carlo! . . . In the Casino the other day I saw . . .'

'Who's the gentleman?' Mark asked, not to be diverted. 'Her son?'

'Her son?' said Roseau, 'Good Heavens, no! That's her gigolo.'

'Her – what did you say?'

'Her gigolo,' explained Roseau coldly. 'Don't you know what a gigolo is? They exist in London, I assure you. She keeps him – he makes love to her, I know all about it because their room's next to mine.'

'Oh!' muttered Mark. He began to sip his aperitif hastily.

'I love your name anyway,' he said, changing the conversation abruptly – 'It suits you.'

'Yes, it suits me – it means a reed,' said Roseau. She had a queer smile – a little sideways smile. Mark wasn't quite sure that he liked it – 'A reed shaken by the wind. That's my motto, that is – are you going? Yes, I'll come to tea soon – sometime: goodbye!'

'He's running off to tell his wife how right she was about

me,' thought Roseau, watching him. 'How rum some English people are! They ask to be shocked and long to be shocked and hope to be shocked, but if you really shock them . . . how shocked they are!'

She finished her aperitif gloomily. She was waiting for an American acquaintance who was calling to take her to lunch. Meanwhile the voices of Fifi and the gigolo grew louder.

'I tell you,' said the gigolo, 'that I must go to Nice this afternoon. It is necessary – I am forced.'

His voice was apologetic but sullen, with a hint of the bully. The male straining at his bonds.

'But, mon chéri,' implored Fifi, 'may I not come with you? We will take tea at the Negresco afterwards.'

The gigolo was sulkily silent. Obviously the Negresco with Fifi did not appeal to him.

She gave way at once.

'Marie!' she called, 'serve Monsieur immediately. Monsieur must catch the one-thirty to Nice. . . . You will return to dinner, my Pierrot?' she begged huskily.

'I think so, I will see,' answered the gigolo loftily, following up his victory as all good generals should – and at that moment Roseau's American acquaintance entered the restaurant.

They lunched on the terrace of a villa looking down on the calmly smiling sea.

'That blue, that blue!' sighed Miss Ward, for such was the American lady's name – 'I always say that blue's wonderful. It gets right down into one's soul – don't you think, Mr Wheeler?'

Mr Wheeler turned his horn spectacles severely on the blue.

'Very fine,' he said briefly.

'I'm sure,' thought Roseau, 'that he's wondering how much it would sell for – bottled.'

She found herself thinking of a snappy advertisement: 'Try our Bottled Blue for Soul Ills.'

Then pulling herself together she turned to Mr Leroy, the fourth member of the party, who was rapidly becoming sulky.

Monsieur Leroy was what the French call 'un joli garçon' – he was even, one might say, a very pretty boy indeed – tall, broad, tanned, clean looking as any Anglo-Saxon. Yet for quite three-quarters of an hour two creatures of the female sex had taken not the faintest notice of him. Monsieur Leroy was puzzled, incredulous. Now he began to be annoyed.

However, he responded instantly to Roseau's effort to include him in the conversation.

'Oh, Madame,' he said, 'I must say that very strong emotion is an excuse for anything – one is mad for the moment.'

'There!' said Roseau in triumph, for the argument had been about whether anything excused the Breaking of Certain Rules.

'That's all nonsense,' said Mr Wheeler.

'But you excuse a sharp business deal?' persisted Roseau.

'Business,' said Mr Wheeler, as if speaking to a slightly idiotic child, 'is quite different, Miss . . . er. . . .'

'You think that,' argued Roseau, 'because it's your form of emotion.'

Mr Wheeler gave her up.

'Maurice,' said Miss Ward, who loved peace, to the young Frenchman, 'fetch the gramophone, there's a good child!'

The gramophone was fetched and the strains of 'Lady, be Good' floated out towards the blue.

The hotel seemed sordid that night to Roseau, full of gentlemen in caps and loudly laughing females. There were large lumps of garlic in the food, the wine was sour. . . . She felt very tired, bruised, aching, yet dull as if she had been defeated in some fierce struggle.

'Oh God, I'm going to think, don't let me think,' she prayed.

For two weeks she had desperately fought off thoughts. She drank another glass of wine, looked at Fifi sitting alone at the mimosa-decorated table with protruding eyes fixed on the door; then looked away again as though the sight frightened her. Her dinner finished she went straight up into her bedroom, took three cachets of veronal, undressed, lay down with the sheet over her head.

Suddenly she got up, staggered against the table, said 'Damn', turned the light on and began to dress, but quietly, quietly. Out through the back door. And why was she dressing anyway? Never mind – done now. And who the hell was that knocking?

It was Fifi. She was wonderfully garbed in a transparent nightgown of a vivid rose colour trimmed with yellow lace. Over this she had hastily thrown a dirty dressing-gown, knotting the sleeves round her neck.

She stared at Roseau, her eyes full of a comic amazement.

'I hope I do not disturb you, Madame,' she said politely. 'But I heard you – enfin – I was afraid that you were ill. My room is next door.'

'Is it?' said Roseau faintly. She felt giddy and clutched at the corner of the table.

'You are surely not thinking of going out now,' Fifi remarked. 'I think it is almost midnight, and you do not look well, Madame.'

She spoke gently, coaxingly, and put her hand on Roseau's arm.

Roseau collapsed on the bed in a passion of tears.

'Ma petite,' said Fifi with decision, 'you will be better in bed, believe me. Where is your chemise de nuit? Ah!'

She took it from the chair close by, looked rapidly with a calculating eye at the lace on it, then put a firm hand on Roseau's skirt to help her with the process of undressing.

'La,' she said, giving the pillow a pat, 'and here is your pocket handkerchief.'

She was not dismayed, contemptuous or curious. She was comforting.

'To cry is good,' she remarked after a pause. 'But not too much. Can I get anything for you, my little one? Some hot milk with rum in it?'

'No, no,' said Roseau, clutching the flannel sleeve, 'don't go – don't leave me – lonely – '

She spoke in English, but Fifi responding at once to the appeal answered:

'Pauvre chou – va,' and bent down to kiss her.

It seemed to Roseau the kindest, the most understanding kiss she had ever had, and comforted she watched Fifi sit on the foot of the bed and wrap her flannel dressing-gown more closely round her. Mistily she imagined that she was a child again and that this was a large, protecting person who would sit there till she slept.

The bed creaked violently under the lady's weight.

'Cursed bed,' muttered Fifi. 'Everything in this house is broken, and then the prices they charge! It is shameful. . . .'

'I am very unhappy,' remarked Roseau in French in a small, tired voice. Her swollen eyelids were half shut.

'And do you think I have not seen?' said Fifi earnestly, laying one plump hand on Roseau's knee. 'Do you think I don't know when a women is unhappy? – I – Besides, with you it is easy to see. You look avec les yeux d'une biche – It's naturally a man who makes you unhappy?'

'Yes,' said Roseau. To Fifi she could tell everything – Fifi was as kind as God.

'Ah! le salaud: ah! le monstre.' This was said mechanically, without real indignation. 'Men are worth nothing. But why should he make you unhappy? He is perhaps jealous?'

'Oh, no!' said Roseau.

'Then perhaps he is méchant – there are men like that – or perhaps he is trying to disembarrass himself of you.'

'That's it,' said Roseau. 'He is trying to – disembarrass himself of me.'

'Ah!' said Fifi wisely. She leant closer. 'Mon enfant,' said she hoarsely, 'do it first. Kick him at the door with a coup de pied quelque part.'

'But I haven't got a door,' said Roseau in English, beginning to laugh hysterically. 'No vestige of a door I haven't – no door, no house, no friends, no money, no nothing.'

'Comment?' said Fifi suspiciously. She disliked foreign languages being talked in her presence.

'Supposing I do – what then?' Roseau asked her.

'What then?' screamed Fifi. 'You ask what then – you who are pretty. If I were in your place I would not ask "what then", I tell you – I should find a chic type – and quickly!'

'Oh!' said Roseau. She was beginning to feel drowsy.

'Un clou chasse l'autre,' remarked Fifi, rather gloomily. 'Yes, that is life – one nail drives out the other nail.'

She got up.

'One says that.' Her eyes were melancholy. 'But when one is caught it is not so easy. No, I adore my Pierrot. I adore that child – I would give him my last sou – and how can he love me? I am old, I am ugly. Oh, I know. Regarde moi ces yeux là!' She pointed to the caverns under her eyes – 'Et ça!' She touched her enormous chest. 'Pierrot who only loves slim women. Que voulez-vous?'

Fifi's shrug was wonderful!

'I love him – I bear everything. But what a life! What a life! . . . You, my little one, a little courage – we will try to find you a chic type, a – '

She stopped seeing that Roseau was almost asleep. 'Alors – I am going – sleep well.'

Next morning Roseau, with a dry tongue, a heavy head, woke to the sound of loud voices in the next room.

Fifi, arguing, grumbling finally weeping – the gigolo who had obviously just come in, p[illegible]sting, becoming surly.

'Menteur, menteur, you ha[illegible]n with a woman!'

'I tell you no. You make ideas for yourself.'

Sobs, kisses, a reconciliation.

'Oh Lord! Oh Lord!' said Roseau. She put the friendly sheet over her head thinking: 'I must get out of this place.'

But when an hour afterwards the stout lady knocked and made her appearance she was powdered, smiling and fresh – almost conventional.

'I hope you slept well last night, Madame; I hope you feel better this morning? Can I do anything for you?'

'Yes, sit and talk to me,' said Roseau. 'I'm not getting up this morning.'

'You are right,' Fifi answered. 'That reposes, a day in bed.' She sat heavily down and beamed. 'And then you must amuse yourself a little,' she advised. 'Distract yourself. If you wish I will show you all the places where one amuses oneself in Nice.'

But Roseau, who saw the 'chic type' lurking in Fifi's eyes, changed the conversation. She said she wished she had something to read.

'I will lend you a book,' said Fifi at once. 'I have many books.'

She went to her room and came back with a thin volume.

'Oh, poetry!' said Roseau. She had hoped for a good detective story. She did not feel in the mood for French poetry.

'I adore poetry,' said Fifi with sentiment. 'Besides, this is very beautiful. You understand French perfectly? Then listen.'

She began to read:

'Dans le chemin libre de mes années
Je marchais fière et je me suis arrêtée. . . .

. . . .

'Thou hast bound my ankles with silken cords.

. . . .

'Que j'oublie les mots qui ne disent pas mon amour,
Les gestes qui ne doivent pas t'enlacer,
Que l'horizon se ferme à ton sourire. . . .

. . . .

'Mais je t'en conjure, ô Sylvius, comme la plus humble des choses qui ont une place dans ta maison – garde-moi.'

In other words: you won't be rotten – now. Will you, will you? I'll do anything you like, but be kind to me, won't you, won't you?

Not that it didn't sound better in French.

'Now,' read Fifi,

'I can walk lightly for I have laid my life in the hands of my lover.

. . . .

'Chante, chante ma vie, aux mains de mon amant!'

. . . .

And so on, and so on.

Roseau thought that it was horrible to hear this ruin of a woman voicing all her own moods, all her own thoughts. Horrible.

> *'Sylvius, que feras-tu à travers les jours de cet*
> *être que t'abandonne sa faiblesse?*
> *Il peut vivre d'un sourire, mourir d'une parole.*
> *Sylvius, qu'en feras-tu?'*

'Have you got any detective stories?' Roseau interrupted suddenly. She felt that she could not bear any more.

Fifi was surprised but obliging. Yes – she had Arsène Lupin, several of Gaston Leroux; also she had 'Shaerlock 'Olmes'.

Roseau chose *Le Fantôme de l'Opéra*, and when Fifi had left the room, stared for a long time at the same page:

'Sylvius, qu'en feras-tu?'

Suddenly she started to laugh and she laughed long, and very loudly for Roseau, who had a small voice and the ghost of a laugh.

That afternoon Roseau met Sylvius, *alias* the gigolo, in the garden of the hotel.

She had made up her mind to detest him. What excuse for the gigolo? None – none whatever.

There he was with his mistress in Cannes and his mistress in Nice. And Fifi on the rack. Fifi, with groans, producing a billet de mille when the gigolo turned the screw. Horrible gigolo!

She scowled at him, carefully thinking out a gibe about the colour of his face powder. But that afternoon his face was unpowdered and reluctantly she was forced to see that the creature was handsome. There was nothing of the blonde beast about the gigolo – he was dark, slim, beautiful as some Latin god. And how soft his eyes were, how sweet his mouth. . . .

Horrible, horrible gigolo!

He did not persist, but looking rather surprised at her snub, went away with a polite murmur: 'Alors, Madame.'

A week later he disappeared.

Fifi in ten days grew ten years older and she came no more to Roseau's room to counsel rum and hot milk instead of veronal. But head up, she faced a hostile and sneering world.

'Have you any news of Monsieur Rivière?' the patronne of the hotel would ask with a little cruel female smile.

'Oh, yes, he is very well,' Fifi would answer airily, knowing perfectly well that the patronne had already examined her letters carefully. 'His grandmother, alas! is much worse, poor woman.'

For the gigolo had chosen the illness of his grandmother as a pretext for his abrupt departure.

One day Fifi despatched by post a huge wreath of flowers – it appeared that the gigolo's grandmother had departed this life.

Then silence. No thanks for the flowers.

Fifi's laugh grew louder and hoarser, and she gave up Vichy for champagne.

She was no longer alone at her table – somehow she could collect men – and as she swam into the room like a big vessel with all sails set, three, four, five would follow in her wake, the party making a horrible noise.

'That dreadful creature!' said Peggy Olsen one night. 'How does she get all those men together?'

Mark laughed and said: 'Take care, she's a pal of Roseau's.'

'Oh! is she?' said Mrs Olsen. She disliked Roseau and thought the hotel with its clientèle of chauffeurs – and worse – beyond what an English gentlewoman should be called upon to put up with.

She was there that night because her husband had insisted on it.

'The girl's lonely – come on, Peggy – don't be such a wet blanket.'

So Peggy had gone, her tongue well sharpened, ready for the fray.

'The dear lady must be very rich,' she remarked. 'She's certainly most hospitable.'

'Oh, she isn't the hostess,' said Roseau, absurdly anxious that her friend's triumph should be obvious. 'The man with the beard is host, I'm sure. He adores Fifi.'

'Extraordinary!' said Mrs Olsen icily.

Roseau thought: 'You sneering beast, you little sneering beast. Fifi's worth fifty of you!' – but she said nothing, contenting herself with one of those sideway smiles which made people think: 'She's a funny one.'

The electric light went out.

The thin, alert, fatigued-looking bonne brought candles. That long drab room looked ghostly in the flickering light – one had an oddly definite impression of something sinister and dangerous – all these heavy jowls and dark, close-set eyes, coarse hands, loud, quarrelsome voices. Fifi looked sinister too with her vital hair and ruined throat.

'You know,' Roseau said suddenly, 'you're right. My hotel is a rum place.'

'Rum is a good word,' said Mark Olsen. 'You really oughtn't to stay here.'

'No, I'm going to leave. It's just been sheer laziness to make the move and my room is rather charming. There's a big mimosa tree just outside the window. But I will leave.'

As the electric light came on again they were discussing the prices of various hotels.

But next morning Roseau, lying in bed and staring at the mimosa tree, faced the thought of how much she would miss Fifi.

It was ridiculous, absurd, but there it was. Just the sound of that hoarse voice always comforted her; gave her the sensation of being protected, strengthened.

'I must be dotty,' said Roseau to herself. 'Of course I would go and like violently someone like that – I must be dotty. No, I'm such a coward, so dead frightened of life, that I must hang on to somebody – even Fifi. . . .'

Dead frightened of life was Roseau, suspended over a dark and terrible abyss – the abyss of absolute loss of self-control.

'Fifi,' said Roseau talking to herself, 'is a pal. She cheers me up. On the other hand she's a dreadful-looking old tart, and I oughtn't to go about with her. It'll be another good old Downward Step if I do.'

Fifi knocked.

She was radiant, bursting with some joyful tidings.

'Pierrot is returning,' she announced.

'Oh!' said Roseau interested.

'Yes, I go to meet him at Nice this afternoon.'

'I am glad!' said Roseau.

It was impossible not to be glad in that large and beaming presence. Fifi wore a new black frock with lace at the neck and wrists and a new hat, a small one.

'My hat?' she asked anxiously. 'Does it make me ridiculous? Is it too small? Does it make me look old?'

'No,' said Roseau, considering her carefully – 'I like it, but put the little veil down.'

Fifi obeyed.

'Ah, well,' she sighed, 'I was always ugly. When I was small my sister called me the devil's doll. Yes – always the compliments like that are what I get. Now – alas! You are sure I am not ridiculous in that hat?'

'No, no,' Roseau told her. 'You look very nice.'

Dinner that night was a triumph for Fifi – champagne flowed – three bottles of it. An enormous bunch of mimosa and carnations almost hid the table from view. The patronne looked sideways, half enviously; the patron chuckled, and the gigolo seemed pleased and affable.

Roseau drank her coffee and smoked a cigarette at the festive table, but refused to accompany them to Nice. They were going to a boîte de nuit, 'all that was of the most chic.'

'Ah bah!' said Fifi good-naturedly scornful, 'she is droll the little one. She always wishes to hide in a corner like a little mouse.'

'No one,' thought Roseau, awakened at four in the morning, 'could accuse Fifi of being a little mouse.' Nothing of the mouse about Fifi.

'I'm taking him to Monte Carlo,' the lady announced next morning. She pronounced it Monte Carl'.

'Monte Carlo – why?'

'He wishes to go. Ah! la la – it will cost me something!' She made a little rueful, clucking noise. 'And Pierrot, who always gives such large tips to the waiters – if he knew as I do what salauds are the garçons de café – '

'Well, enjoy yourself,' Roseau said laughing. 'Have a good time.'

The next morning she left the hotel early and did not return till dinnertime, late, preoccupied.

As she began her meal she noticed that some men in the restaurant were jabbering loudly in Italian – but they always jabbered.

The patron was not there – the patronne, looking haughty, was talking rapidly to her lingère.

But the bonne looked odd, Roseau thought, frightened but bursting with importance. As she reached the kitchen she called in a shrill voice to the cook: 'It is in the *Éclaireur*. Have you seen?'

Roseau finished peeling her apple. Then she called out to the patronne – she felt impelled to do it.

'What is it, Madame? Has anything happened?'

The patronne hesitated.

'Madame Carly – Madame Fifi – has met with an accident,' she answered briefly.

'An accident? An automobile accident? Oh, I do hope it isn't serious.'

'It's serious enough – assez grave,' the patronne answered evasively.

Roseau asked no more questions. She took up the *Éclaireur de Nice* lying on the table and looked through it.

She was looking for the 'Fatal Automobile Accident'.

She found the headline:

YET ANOTHER DRAMA OF JEALOUSY

'Madame Francine Carly, aged 48, of 7 rue Notre Dame des Pleurs, Marseilles, was fatally stabbed last night at the hotel —, Monte Carlo, by her lover Pierre Rivière, aged 24, of rue Madame Tours. Questioned by the police he declared that he acted in self-defence as his mistress, who was of a very jealous temperament, had attacked him with a knife when told of his approaching marriage, and threatened to blind him. When the proprietor of the hotel, alarmed by the woman's shrieks, entered the room accompanied by two policemen, Madame Carly was lying unconscious, blood streaming from the wounds in her throat. She was taken to the hospital, where she died without recovering consciousness.

'The murderer has been arrested and taken to the Depôt.'

Roseau stared for a long time at the paper.

'I must leave this hotel,' was her only thought, and she slept soundly that night without fear of ghosts.

A horrible, sordid business. Poor Fifi! Almost she hated herself for feeling so little regret.

But next morning while she was packing she opened the book of poems, slim, much handled, still lying on the table, and searched for the verse Fifi had read:

> '*Maintenant je puis marcher légère,*
> *J'ai mis toute ma vie aux mains de mon amant.*
> *Chante, chante ma vie aux mains de mon amant.*'

Suddenly Roseau began to cry.

'O poor Fifi! O poor Fifi!'

In that disordered room in the midst of her packing she cried bitterly, heartbroken.

Till, in the yellow sunshine that streamed into the room, she imagined that she saw her friend's gay and childlike soul, freed from its gross body, mocking her gently for her sentimental tears.

'Oh well!' said Roseau.

She dried her eyes and went on with her packing.

Vienne

FUNNY how it's slipped away, Vienna. Nothing left but a few snapshots.

Not a friend, not a pretty frock – nothing left of Vienna.

Hot sun, my black frock, a hat with roses, music, lots of music –

The little dancer at the Parisien with a Kirchner girl's legs and a little faun's face.

She was so exquisite that girl that it clutched at one, gave one a pain that anything so lovely could ever grow old, or die, or do ugly things.

A fragile child's body, a fluff of black skirt ending far above the knee. Silver straps over that beautiful back, the wonderful legs in black silk stockings and little satin shoes, short hair, cheeky little face.

She gave me the songe bleu. Four, five feet she could jump and come down on that wooden floor without a sound. Her partner, an unattractive individual in badly fitting trousers, could lift her with one hand, throw her in the air – catch her, swing her as one would a flower.

At the end she made an adorable little 'gamine's' grimace.

Ugly humanity, I'd always thought. I saw people differently

afterwards – because for once I'd met sheer loveliness with a flame inside, for there was 'it' – the spark, the flame in her dancing.

Pierre (a damn good judge) raved about her. André also, though cautiously, for he was afraid she would be too expensive.

All the French officers coveted her – night after night the place was packed.

Finally she disappeared. Went back to Budapest where afterwards we heard of her.

Married to a barber. Rum.

Pretty women, lots. How pretty women here are. Lovely food. Poverty gone, the dread of it – going.

'I call them war material,' said Colonel Ishima, giggling.

He meant women, the Viennese women. But when I asked him about the Geisha – I thought it might be amusing to hear about the Geisha first hand as it were, Europeans are so very contradictory about the subject – he pursed up his mouth and looked prim.

'We don't talk about these people – shameful people.'

However, he added after looking suspiciously at a dish of kidneys and asking what they were:

'The Geisha were good people during the war, patriotic people. The Geisha served Nippon well.'

He meant the Russo-Japanese War. One had visions of big blond Russian officers and slant-eyed girls like exotic dolls stabbing them under the fifth rib, or stealing their papers when they were asleep. . . .

Every fortnight the Japanese officers solemnly entertained their following at Sacher's Hotel, and they were entertained one by one in return, because in a mass they were really rather overwhelming.

Of course, there it was – the Japanese had to have a following. To begin with, not one of them could speak the three necessary languages, English, German and French, properly. It meant perpetual translation and arguments. And they were dreadfully afraid of not being as tactful as an Asiatic power ought to be, or of voting with the minority instead of the majority, which would have been the end of them at Tokio.

So Ishima had his secretary and confidential adviser (that was Pierre) and Hato had his, and Matsjijiri had his, not to speak of three typists, a Hungarian interpreter and various other hangers-on.

Every fortnight they gave a dinner to the whole lot. It began with caviare and ended with Tokayer and Hato singing love songs, which was the funniest thing I ever heard.

He only had one eye, poor dear; the other disappeared during the Russo-Japanese War. He sang in a high bleat, holding tightly on to one foot and rocking backwards and forwards.

He was very vieux jeu, arrièrē, a Samurai or something, he wore a kimono whenever he could get into it and he loved making solemn proclamations to the delegation. He called them: Ordres du jour.

He made one to the typists, à propos of the temptation of Vienna, which began like this:

'Vous êtes jeunes, vous êtes femmes, vous êtes faibles. Pour l'honneur du Nippon,' etc, etc.

Through some mistake this ordre du jour was solemnly brought to an elderly, moustached French general, whilst the Commission was having a meeting to decide some minor detail of the fate of the conquered country. He opened it and read: 'Vous êtes jeunes, vous êtes femmes, vous êtes faibles.'

'Merde, alors!' said the general, 'qu'est-ce que c'est que ça?'

Hato was a great joy. He despised Europeans heartily. They all did that, exception made in favour of Germany – for the

Japanese thought a lot of the German Army and the German way of keeping women in their place. They twigged that at once. Not much they didn't twig.

But they were all bursting with tact and Ishima, immediately after his remark about war material, paid me many flowery compliments. He hoped, he said, to see me one day in Japan. The Lord forbid!

After dinner we went to the Tabarin. He stared haughtily with boot-button eyes at a very pretty little girl, a girl like a wax doll, who was strolling aimlessly about, and who smiled at him very pitifully and entreatingly when she thought I was not looking.

I knew all about her. She had been Ishima's friend, his acknowledged friend – en titre. She really was pretty and young. The odd thing is that the Japanese have such good taste in European women, whereas European taste in Japanese women is simply atrocious, or so the Japanese say.

Well, and Ishima had got rid of her because she was faithful to him. Odd reason.

It happened like this: he had a visit from a friend from Japan – a prince of the blood, who adored plain boiled fish and ate them in a simple and efficient way, holding them up by the tail with one hand and using his fork vigorously with the other. Ishima offered him with eastern hospitality everything he possessed – his suite of rooms at the Sacher and the services of his little friend. But the little friend, thinking perhaps to enhance her value, objected – objected with violence, made a scene in fact, and Ishima, more in sorrow than anger, never saw her again.

He just couldn't get over it.

Pierre told me that one day, after meditating for a long time, he asked: 'Was she mad, poor girl, or would others have done the same?'

Pierre answered cautiously that it depended. The ones with temperament would all have made a fuss if only for pride's sake, and the Viennese have nearly as much temperament as the French, the Hungarians even more. On the other hand, the Germans – enfin, it depended.

Ishima meditated a long time. Then he shook his head and said: 'Tiens, tiens, c'est bizarre!' . . .

I thought of the story that night and hated him. He was so like a monkey, and a fattish monkey which was worse. . . .

On the other hand there was Kashua, who looked even more like a monkey and he was a chic type who had rescued another unfortunate bit of war material deserted without a penny by an Italian officer. Not only did Kashua give her a fabulous sum in yen, but also he paid her expenses at a sanatorium for six months – she was consumptive.

There you are! How can one judge!

Kashua came up grinning and bowing and sat with us. He showed me photographs of his wife – she looked a darling – and of his three daughters. Their names meant: Early Rising, Order, and Morning Sun. And he had bought them each a typewriter as a present.

Then, with tears in his eyes and a quaver of pride in his voice – his little son.

'I think your wife is very pretty,' I told him.

He said, grinning modestly: 'Not at all, not at all.'

'And I am sure she will be very happy when you will go back to Japan,' I said.

'Very happy, very happy,' he told me. 'Madame Kashua is a most happy woman, a very fortunate woman.'

I said: 'I expect she is.'

Well, Kashua is a chic type, so I expect she is too.

But I believe my dislike of the Viennese nightplaces started at that moment.

We soon found a flat – the top floor of General von Marken's house in the Razunoffskygasse, and André shared it with us for a time.

He was a little man, his legs were too short, but he took the greatest trouble to have his suits cut to disguise it.

I mean, with the waist of his coat very high, almost under the arms, the chest padded, decided heels to his shoes.

After all these pains what Tilly called his 'silhouette' was not unattractive.

One could tell a Frenchman, Parisian, a mile off. Quantities of hair which he had waved every week, rather honest blue eyes, a satyr's nose and mouth.

That's what André was, a satyr – aged twenty-four.

He'd stiffen all over when he saw a pretty woman, like those dogs – don't they call them pointers – do when they see a rabbit. His nose would go down over his mouth.

It was the oddest thing to watch him at the Tabarin when there was a particularly good dancer.

He spent hours, all his spare time, I believe, pursuing, searching.

One day walking in the Kärntnerstrasse we saw the whole proceeding – the chase, the hat raising, the snub. He often got snubbed.

He was so utterly without pretence or shame that he wasn't horrid.

He lived for women; his father had died of women and so would he. Voilà tout.

When I arrived in Vienna his friend was a little dancer called Lysyl.

Lysyl and Ossi was her turn – an Apache dance.

She had a wonderfully graceful body, and a brutal peasant's face – and André was torn between a conviction that she wasn't 'chic' enough and a real appreciation of the said grace – he'd lean over the loge when she was dancing, breathing, hard eyes popping out of his head.

One night we went with him to some out-of-the-way music-hall to see her, and after her turn was over she came to visit our loge – on her best behaviour of course.

I took a sudden fancy to her that night – to her grace and her little child's voice saying: 'Ach, meine blumen – André, André. Ich hab' meine blumen vergessen' – so I snubbed André when he started to apologize, I suppose for contaminating me, and told him of course he could bring her back to supper.

We squashed up together in one of those Viennese cabs with two horses that go like hell. She sat in a big coat and little hat, hugging her blumen – in the dark one couldn't see her brute's face.

She really was charming that night.

But next morning, when she came to say goodbye before going, the charm wasn't at all in evidence.

She took half my box of cigarettes, asked by signs how much my dress had cost, 'Why is this woman polite to me,' said her little crafty eyes.

Also, most unlucky of all, she met Blanca von Marken on the stairs.

An hour afterwards Madame von Marken had come to see me, to protest.

Blanca was a jeune fille. Surely I understood. . . . I would forgive her, but in Vienna they were old-fashioned. . . .

Of course I understood, and against all my sense of fairness and logic apologized and said I agreed.

For God knows, if there's one hypocrisy I loathe more than another, it's the fiction of the 'good' woman and the 'bad' one.

André apologized too, but I'm sure he had no sense of being wanting in logic.

So he grovelled with gusto, feeling chivalrous as he did so, and a protector of innocence. Oh, Lord!

'Vous savez, mon vieux, je n'ai pas pensé – une jeune fille!'

However, not being Don Quixote I did not even try to protect Lysyl.

I think she could take care of herself.

But though she got on as a dancer and became mondäne Tänzerin – I think that's how they spell it – André was done with her.

The fiat had gone forth.

Elle n'a pas de chic.

Because I liked Blanca and Madame von Marken, I even tried to make up for the shock to their virtue by hanging up Franz Josef and all the ancestors in the sitting-room.

I'd taken them all down in an effort to make the place less gloomy and whiskery and antimacassary – but I saw that it hurt that poor pretty lady so up they went again and I started living in my bedroom, which was charming.

Very big, polished floor, lots of windows, little low tables to make coffee – some lovely Bohemian glass.

Also I spent much time in the Prater.

Quantities of lilac, mauve and white –

Always now I'll associate lilac with Vienna.

The Radetzky Hotel was perhaps twenty minutes or half an hour from Vienna by car – and it was real country.

But that is one of the charms of the place – no suburbs.

It wasn't really comfortable; there wasn't a bathroom in the whole establishment, but for some reason it was exciting and gay and they charged enormous prices accordingly.

All the men who made money out of the 'change came there to spend it, bringing the woman of the moment.

All the pretty people with doubtful husbands or no husbands, or husbands in jail (lots of men went to jail – I don't wonder. Every day new laws about the exchange and smuggling gold).

Everybody, in fact.

Very vulgar, of course, but all Vienna was vulgar.

Gone the 'Aristokraten'.

They sat at home rather hungry, while their women did the washing.

The ugly ones.

The pretty ones tried to get jobs as mondäne Tänzerinen.

Quite right too – perhaps.

Just prejudice to notice podgy hands and thick ankles – keep your eyes glued on the pretty face.

Also prejudice to see stark brutality behind the bows and smiles of the men.

Also prejudice to watch them eat or handle a toothpick.

Stupid too – so much better not to look.

The girls were well dressed, not the slightest bit made up – that seemed odd after Paris.

Gorgeous blue sky and green trees and a good orchestra.

And heat and heat.

I was cracky with joy of life that summer of 1921.

I'd darling muslin frocks covered with frills and floppy hats – or a little peasant dress and no hat.

Well, and Tillie was a queen of the Radetzky. It was through her (she told André) that we got to know of it.

Tillie possessed wonderful eyes, grey-blue – hair which made her look like Gaby Deslys, a graceful figure.

And with that she made one entirely forget a dreadful complexion, four gold teeth, and enormous feet.

This sounds impossible in a place where competition was, to say the least of it, keen, but is strictly true.

Every time one saw Tillie one would think – 'Gee, how pretty she is.' In the midst of all the others everyone would turn to look at her and her gorgeous hair.

And behind walked André, caught at last, held tight 'by the skin', as the French say.

All his swank was gone – he watched her as a dog watches his master, and when he spoke to her his voice was like a little boy's.

She'd flirt outrageously with somebody else (half the men there had been her lovers so it was an exciting renewal of old acquaintanceships), and André would sit so miserable that the tears were nearly there.

One night in fact they did come when I patted him on the arm and said 'Poor old André – cheer up.'

'Une grue,' said Pierre brutally. 'André is a fool – and Frances, leave that girl alone – '

But I didn't leave her alone at once, too interested to watch the comedy.

Next Saturday evening we were dining at Radetzky with a German acquaintance of Pierre's.

Excessively good-looking, but, being a Prussian, brutal, of course.

'Donner-r-r- wetter-r-r-' he'd bawl at the waiters, and the poor men would jump and run.

But perhaps I exaggerated the brutality for he'd done something I'm still English enough to loathe: he'd discussed Tillie with great detail and openness – he'd had a love affair with her.

Just as we were talking about something else, herself and André hove in sight.

André walked straight to our table and asked if they might join us.

Impossible to refuse without being brutal, though Pierre wasn't cordial, and the other man kissed her hand with a sneer that gave the whole show away.

As for Tillie, she behaved perfectly – not a movement, not the flicker of an eyelash betrayed her – though it must have been trying, just as she was posing as a mondaine, to meet this enemy openly hostile.

Nor did she let it interfere in the slightest with her little plan for the evening, well thought out, well carried out.

She owned a beautiful pearl necklace which she always wore, and that night she firmly led the conversation in the direction of pearls.

I couldn't do much 'leading', or indeed much talking in German. I gathered the drift of things, and occasionally Pierre translated.

Tillie's pearls (she told us) were all she had left of a marvellous stock of jewels (wunderschön!).

In fact, all she had between herself and destitution, all and all –

Ach – the music chimed in a mournful echo. . . .

She was sad that evening, subdued, eyes almost black, voice sweet and quivery.

After dinner she asked me charmingly if I would mind 'a little walking' – it was so hot – they weren't playing well.

I was quite ready – it was hot – and Tillie went up to her room and came down with a scarf very tightly wrapped round her throat.

We set out. Myself, Pierre and Lieutenant – I've completely forgotten his name – walking together, André and Tillie some little way in front.

Pitch dark in the woods round the hotel – so dark that it frightened me after a while, and I suggested going back.

Shouted to the others, no answer, too far ahead.

We'd got back and were sitting comfortably in the hall drinking liqueurs (alone, for everybody assembled in the bar after dinner to dance) when André came in running, out of breath, agitated.

'The pearls, Tillie's pearls, lost – Bon Dieu de bon Dieu. She's dropped them – '

He spoke to me, the only sympathetic listener.

Then entered Tillie. Gone the pathos. She looked ugly and dangerous, with her underlip thrust out.

A torrent of German to Pierre who listened and said in a non-committal way: 'She says that André kissed her in the woods and was rough, and that the clasp of the pearls wasn't sure. It's André's fault, she says, and he'll have to pay up.'

The other man laughed. Suddenly she turned on him like a fury.

'Mein lieber Herr . . .' I couldn't understand the words; I did the tone.

'Mind your own business if you know what's good for yourself.'

Meanwhile Pierre, whose instinct is usually to act while other people talk, had gone off and come back with two lanterns and a very sensible proposition.

We would go at once, all four of us, holding hands so that not an inch of the ground should be missed, over exactly the same road.

Too dark for anyone else to have picked them up.

Tillie, to my astonishment, didn't seem very keen.

However, we set out in a long row stooping forward. André held one lantern, Pierre the other.

I looked at first perfectly seriously, straining my eyes.

Then André moved his lantern suddenly and I saw Tillie's face. She was smiling, I could swear – she certainly wasn't looking on the ground.

I looked at Pierre – his search was very perfunctory; the other man wasn't even pretending to look.

At that moment I liked André – I felt sorry for him, akin to him.

He and I of the party had both swallowed the story; we were the Fools.

I could have shaken his hand and said: 'Hail, brother Doormat, in a world of Boots.'

But I'd been too sure of the smile to go on looking.

After that I gave all my attention to the little game the German was playing with my hand.

He'd reached my wrist – my arm – I pulled away –

My hand again, but the fingers interlocked.

Very cool and steady his was – and a tiny pulse beating somewhere.

A dispute. We didn't come this way Tillie was saying.

But it had become a farce to everybody but the faithful André.

We went back, but before we'd come within hearing of the music from the hotel, he had comforted her with many promises.

And he kept them too. He turned a deaf ear to all hints that it was or might be a trick.

When we went to Budapest Tillie came. Later on to Berlin, she went too.

She never left him till she could arrange to do so, taking with her every sou he possessed, and a big diamond he'd bought.

This sequel we heard only later.

Poor André! Let us hope he had some compensation for

forgetting for once that 'eat or be eaten' is the inexorable law of life.

The next girl, perhaps, will be sweet and gentle. His turn to be eater.

Detestable world.

Simone and Germaine, two of the typists at the delegation, were having a succès fou. Simone at least deserved it.

She specialized in English, Americans and French.

Germaine on the other hand had a large following among the Italians, Greeks, and even a stray Armenian who (she said) had offered her fifty thousand francs for one night.

Simone was sublimely conceited.

She told me once that Captain La Croix had called her the quintessence of French charm, Flemish beauty and Egyptian mystery. (She was born in Cairo, French mother, Belgian father.)

Both girls looked at me a little warily, but they were too anxious to keep in with Pierre to be anything but polite. I'd noticed people growing more and more deferential to Pierre, and incidentally to me. I'd noticed that he seemed to have money – a good deal – a great deal.

He made it on the 'change, he told me.

Then one day in the spring of 1921 we left the flat in Razunoffskygasse for rooms in the Imperial.

We sent off the cook and D—, promoted to be my maid, came with us.

Nice to have lots of money – nice, nice. Goody to have a car, a chauffeur, rings, and as many frocks as I liked.

Good to have money, money. All the flowers I wanted. All the compliments I wanted. Everything, everything.

Oh, great god money – you make possible all that's nice in life. Youth and beauty, the envy of women, and the love of men.

Even the luxury of a soul, a character and thoughts of one's own you give, and only you. To look in the glass and think I've got what I wanted.

I gambled when I married and I've won.

As a matter of fact I wasn't so exalted really, but it was exceedingly pleasant.

Spending and spending. And there was always more.

One day I had a presentiment.

Pierre gave an extra special lunch to the Japanese officers, Shogun, Hato, Ishima and Co.

We lunched in a separate room, which started my annoyance, for I preferred the restaurant, especially with the Japanese, who depressed me.

It was rather cold and dark and the meal seemed interminable.

Shogun in the intervals of eating enormously told us a long history of an officer in Japan who 'hara-kari'd' because his telephone went wrong during manœuvres.

Rotten reason I call it, but Shogun seemed to think him a hero.

Escaped as soon as I could upstairs.

I was like Napoleon's mother, suddenly: 'Provided it lasts.'

And if it does not? Well, thinking that was to feel the authentic 'cold hand clutching my heart'.

And a beastly feeling too – let me tell you.

So damned well I knew that I could never be poor again with courage or dignity.

I did a little sum; translated what we were spending into francs – into pounds – I was appalled. (When we first arrived in Vienna the crown was thirteen to the franc – at that time it was about sixty.)

As soon as I could I attacked Pierre.

First he laughed, then he grew vexed.

Frances, I tell you it's all right. How much am I making? A lot.

How much exactly? Can't say. How? You won't understand.

Don't be frightened, it – brings bad luck. You'll stop my luck.

I shut up. I know so well that presentiments, fears, are unlucky.

'Don't worry,' said Pierre, 'soon I will pull it quite off and we will be rich, rich.'

We dined in a little corner of the restaurant.

At the same table a few days before we came, a Russian girl twenty-four years of age had shot herself.

With her last money she had a decent meal and then bang! Out –

And I made up my mind that if ever it came to it I should do it too.

Not to be poor again. No and No and No.

So darned easy to plan that – and always at the last moment – one is afraid. Or cheats oneself with hope.

I can still do this and this. I can still clutch at that or that.

So-and-So will help me.

How you fight, cleverly and well at first, then more wildly – then hysterically.

I can't go down, I won't go down. Help me, help me!

Steady – I must be clever. So-and-So will help.

But So-and-So smiles a worldly smile.

You get nervous. He doesn't understand, I'll make him –

But So-and-So's eyes grow cold. You plead.

Can't you help me, won't you, please? It's like this and this –

So-and-So becomes uncomfortable; obstinate.

No good.

I mustn't cry, I won't cry.

And that time you don't. You manage to keep your head up, a smile on your face.

So-and-So is vastly relieved. So relieved that he offers at once the little help that is a mockery, and the consoling compliment.

In the taxi still you don't cry.

You've thought of someone else.

But at the fifth or sixth disappointment you cry more easily.

After the tenth you give it up. You are broken – no nerves left.

And every second-rate fool can have their cheap little triumph over you – judge you with their little middle-class judgment.

Can't do anything for them. No good.

C'est rien – c'est une femme qui se noie!

But two years, three years afterwards. Salut to you, little Russian girl, who had pluck enough and knowledge of the world enough, to finish when your good time was over.

The day before we left Vienna for Budapest was thundery and colder.

I'd spent nearly two hours in a massage place the Russian girl had told me of.

The Russian girl was introduced to me to replace Tillie. She had two advantages: a husband, and a slight knowledge of French.

We'd sat up night after night in the Radetzsky bar. (Pierre always gathered swarms of people round him.) The most amusing of the party being an old lady of over seventy who wore a bright yellow wig. She'd been an actress and still had heaps of temperament left.

There she sat night after night, drinking punch and singing about Liebe and Frauen with the best.

I came out of the shop and walked down the strasse – face like a doll's – not a line, not a shadow, eyes nicer than a doll's. Hadn't I had stuff dropped in to make the pupils big and black?

Highly pleased with everything I was that afternoon – with the massage place, with the shortness of my frock, with life in general.

Abruptly the reaction came when I sat down to dinner. I was alone that evening – the presentiment, the black mood, in full swing.

A gentleman with a toothpick gazed fondly at me (in the intervals of serious excavating work), I glued my eyes on my plate.

Oh, abomination of desolation – to sit for two hours being massaged, to stand for hours choosing a dress. All to delight the eyes of the gentleman with the toothpick.

(Who finding me unresponsive has already turned his attention elsewhere.)

I hate him worse than ever.

Franzi is in the hall. The Herr has told him to bring the car and take me for a drive.

Nice Franzi.

I climb in – go quick, Franzi. Schnell – eine andere platz neit Prater neit weg zum Baden – neit Weiner Wald.

This is my German after two years! I mean go fast. Go to a new place, not the Prater, not the way to Baden –

Yes, that night was the last frenzied effort of my guardian angel, poor creature. I've never seen so clearly all my faults and failures and utter futility. I've never had so strong a wish to pack my trunks and clear.

Clear off – different life, different people.

Work.

Go to England – be quite different.

Even clearly and coldly the knowledge that I was not being sincere.

That I didn't want to work.

Or wear ugly clothes.

That for ten years I'd lived like that – and that except for a miracle, I couldn't change.

'Don't want to change,' defiantly.

I've compensations.

Oh, yes, compensations – moments.

No one has more.

'Liar, Liar,' shrieked the angel, 'pack your trunks and clear.'

Poor angel – it was hopeless. You hadn't a chance in that lovely night of Vienne.

Especially as in the midst of it came a terrific bump.

In his zeal to find an andere weg Franzi had taken me along a road that hadn't been repaired since the year dot. We'd gone right over a stone, so big that I jumped, not being solid, a good three feet into the air. Fell back luckily into the car.

Franzi has stopped and looks behind frightened. I tell him to go home.

It's not my fault.

Men have spoilt me – always disdaining my mind and concentrating on my body. Women have spoilt me with their senseless cruelties and stupidities. Can I help it if I've used my only weapon?

Yes, my only one.

Lies everything else – lies –

Lord, how I hate most women here, their false smiles, their ferocious jealousies of each other, their cunning – like animals.

They are animals, probably. Look at all the wise men who think so and have thought so.

Even Jesus Christ was kind but cold and advised having as little as possible to do with them.

Besides, if I went back to London –

I go back to what, to who?

How lonely I am – how lonely I am.

Tears.

Self-pity, says the little thing in my brain coldly, is the most ridiculous and futile of emotions. Go to bed, woman.

I creep in and am comforted. How I adore nice sheets; how good the pillow smells.

I'm awfully happy really – why did I suddenly get the blues?

Tomorrow I'll see Budapest.

Ridiculous idea to go to London. What should I do in London –

Goodbye Vienna, the lilac, the lights looking down from Kahlenberg, the old lady with the yellow wig singing of Frauen.

Will I be ever like that old lady? And run to the massage shop because I have to prop up the failing structure? Possibly, probably.

Lovely Vienna. Never see you again.

Nice linen sheets.

Sleep.

Well, we all have our illusions. God knows it would be difficult to look in the glass without them.

I, that my life from seventeen to twenty-two is responsible for my damned weakness, and Simone that she has the prettiest legs in Paris. Good women that they're not really spiteful, bad ones that they're not really growing older or the latest lover growing colder.

I can't imagine winter in Budapest. Can't imagine it anything else but hot summer.

Heat and a perpetual smell, an all-pervading smell – in the hotels, in the streets, on the river, even outside the town I still imagined I smelt it.

The Hungarians told us it used to be the cleanest city in Europe till the Bolsheviks made it dirty – the Bolsheviks and 'the cursed, the horrible Roumanians'.

It was now being cleaned gradually – very gradually, I should say.

Haughton used to bark loudly (he did bark!) about the exact reasons why it had always been, and still was the most interesting city in Europe, with the exception of Petersburg before the war. 'Les femmes ici ont du chien' – that's how the French officers explained the matter.

Anyway, I liked it – I liked it better than Vienna.

Haughton lived in the same hotel as we did. We took our meals together and every night we made up a party for the Orpheum or one of the dancing places. He generally brought along a bald Italian with kind brown eyes, a sailor, and a Polish woman and her husband.

He was in the Commission because he spoke Russian, German, French, Italian, even a little Hungarian. Marvellous person!

He had lived in Russia for years, tutor or something to one of the Grand Dukes, and I admired his taste in ladies. He liked them slim, frail, graceful, scented, vicious, painted, charming – and he was chic with them from first to last – un-English in fact, though he remained English to look at.

But sometimes he spoilt those perfect nights when we dined outside Buda with his incessant, not very clever cynicisms.

'Ha, ha, ha! Good Lord! Yes. Damn pretty woman. What?'

When the tziganes were playing their maddest and saddest – he'd still go on happily barking. . . .

Budapest looks theatrically lovely from a distance. I remember the moon like a white bird in the afternoon sky; the greyish-green trunks of sycamore trees, the appalling bumps in the road.

'Not too fast, Franzi; don't go too fast!' . . .

Then back to the city and its vivid smells, the wail of tzigane orchestras, the little dancer of the Orpheum – what was her name? . . . Ilonka – nice name, sounds like a stone thrown into deep water. She would come smiling and silent – she could speak neither French nor German – to sit with us when her turn was over.

'Awfully monotonous this tzigane stuff, what?' Haughton would say, fidgeting.

It was, I suppose. It seemed to be endless variations and inversions of a single chord – tuneless, plaintive, melancholy; the wind over the plain, the hungry cry of the human heart and all the rest of it. . . . Well, well. . . .

There was a hard, elegant, little sofa in our room, covered with striped, yellow silk – sky-blue cushions. I spent long afternoons lying on that sofa plunged in a placid dream of maternity.

I felt a calm sense of power lying in that dark, cool room, as though I could inevitably and certainly draw to myself all I had ever wished for in life – as though I were mysteriously irresistible, a magnet, a Femme Sacrée.

One can become absorbed . . . exalted . . . lost as it were, when one is going to have a baby, and one is extremely pleased about it.

One afternoon Pierre said: 'If anyone comes here from the Allgemeine Verkehrsbank you must say that I'm not in and that you don't know when I'll be back.'

Someone called from the Bank – a fat, short man, insisting, becoming rude in bad French. He would see Monsieur. He must see Monsieur. Madame could not say when Monsieur would be back. 'Très bien – très bien.' He would go to Monsieur's office to make inquiries.

He departed. His back looked square, revengeful – catastrophic – that's the word. I believe that looking at the man's back I guessed everything, foresaw everything.

I attacked Pierre as soon as he came home. I mean questioned him – but he was so evasive that I turned it into an attack. Evasion has always irritated me.

'Tell me, for Heaven's sake, have you lost a lot of money, or something? You have. I know you have – you must tell me.'

He said: 'My dear, let me alone, I'll pull it off if you let me alone – but I don't want to talk about it. . . . Haughton has asked us to dine at the Ritz. . . . Et qu'importent les jours pourvu que les nuits soient belles?'

He made a large and theatrical gesture.

I let him alone, weakly, I suppose. But one gets used to security and to thinking of one's husband as a money-maker, a juggler, performing incredible and mysterious feats with yen, with lire, with francs and sterling . . . 'change on Zurich. . . .

I let him alone – but I worried. I caught Haughton looking at me as if he were sorry for me. . . . Sorry for me. Haughton!

Ten days after the man of the Bank had called, I went up to my bedroom at half-past six to change my frock and found Pierre sitting on the striped yellow sofa hunched up, staring at the revolver in his hand.

I always hated revolvers, little, vicious, black things. Just to look at a revolver or a gun gives me a pain deep down in my head; not because they're dangerous – I don't hate knives – but because the noise of a shot hurts my ears.

I said: 'Oh, Pierre, put that thing away! How horribly unkind you are to frighten me!'

Stupid to cry at the very moment one should keep calm.

He was silent, rather surly.

Well, I dragged the truth out of him. He told me, moving

one foot restlessly and looking rather like a schoolboy, that he had lost money – other people's money – the Commission's money – Ishima had let him down. . . .

Then followed the complicated history of yens – of francs – of krönen. He interrupted himself to say: 'You don't understand a thing about money. What is the good of asking me to explain? I'm done, I tell you, tried everything . . . no good! I may be arrested any time now.'

I was calm, cool, overflowing with common sense. I believe people who are badly wounded must be like that before the wound begins to hurt. . . . Now then, what is the best way to stop this bleeding? . . . Bandages. . . . Impossible that this and no other is the shot that is going to finish one. . . .

I sat on the sofa beside him and said: 'Tell me how much you need to put yourself straight? I can understand that much at any rate.'

He told me, and there was a dead silence.

'Leave me alone,' he said. 'Let me put a bullet in my head. You think I want to go to jail in Budapest? I haven't a chance!'

I explained, still calmly and reasonably, that he must not kill himself and leave me alone – that I was frightened – that I did not want to die – that somehow I would find the money to pay his debts.

All the time I was speaking he kept his eyes on the door as if he were watching for it to open suddenly and brutally. Then repeated as if I had not spoken: 'I'm fichu. . . . Go away and let me get out of it the only way I can. . . . I've saved four thousand francs ready money for you. . . . And your rings. . . . Haughton will help you. . . . I'm fichu. . . .'

I set my mouth: 'You aren't. Why can't you be a man and fight?'

'I won't wait here to be arrested,' he answered me sulkily, 'they shan't get me, they shan't get me, I tell you.'

My plan of going to London to borrow money was already complete in my head. One thinks quickly sometimes.

'Don't let's wait then. Pierre, you can't do such a rotten thing as to leave me alone?'

'Mon petit,' he said, 'I'm a damn coward or I would have finished it before. I tell you I'm right – I'm done. Save yourself. . . . You can't save me!'

He laughed with tears in his eyes. 'My poor Francine, wait a bit. . . .'

'Let's go, let's get away,' I said, 'and shut up about killing yourself. If you kill yourself you know what will happen to me?'

We stared at each other.

'You know damn well,' I told him.

He dropped his eyes and muttered: 'All right – all right! . . . Only don't forget I've warned you, I've told you. It's going to be hell. . . . You're going to blame me one day for not getting out quick and leaving you to save yourself.'

He began to walk restlessly up and down the room.

We decided that we could leave early the next morning. Just to go off. Like that. We made plans – suddenly we were speaking in whispers. . . .

We had dinner upstairs that night, I remember – paprika, canard sauvage, two bottles of Pommery.

'Allons, Francine, cheer up! Au mauvais jeu il faut faire bonne mine.'

I've always loved him for these sudden, complete changes of mood. No Englishman could change so suddenly – so completely. I put out my hand, and as I touched him my courage, my calm, my insensibility left me and I felt a sort of vague and bewildered fright. Horrible to feel that henceforth and for ever one would live with the huge machine of law, order, respectability against one. Horrible to be certain that one was not strong enough to fight it.

'Au mauvais jeu bonne mine.' . . . A good poker face, don't they call it? . . . The quality of not getting rattled when anything goes wrong. . . .

When we opened our second bottle of Pommery I had become comfortingly convinced that I was predestined – a feather on the sea of fate and all the rest. And what was the use of worrying – anyway? . . .

As I was drinking a fourth glass, hoping to increase this comforting feeling of irresponsibility, Haughton knocked and came in to see us.

There was a moment that night when I nearly confided in Haughton.

Pierre had gone away to telephone, to see the chauffeur, and I've always liked those big men with rather hard blue eyes. I trust them instinctively – and probably wrongly. I opened my mouth to say: 'Haughton, this and that is the matter. . . . I'm frightened to death, really. . . . What am I to do?'

And as I was hesitating Pierre came back.

At one o'clock we began to pack, making as little noise as possible. We decided to take only one trunk.

I remember the table covered with cigarette ends and liqueur glasses, the two empty bottles of champagne, and the little yellow sofa looking rather astonished and disapproving.

At half-past six in the morning we left the hotel.

That journey to Prague was like a dream. Not a nightmare; running away can be exhilarating but endless as are certain dreams, and unreal.

While I dressed and finished packing my hands had trembled with fright and cold, but before we left Budapest behind us the hunted feeling had vanished.

There is no doubt that running away on a fresh, blue morning can be exhilarating.

I patted the quivering side of the car, gazed at Franzi's stolid back, wondered if he guessed anything, and decided he probably did, sung 'Mit ihrem roten Chapeau'. After all, when one is leaving respectability behind one may as well do it with an air.

The country stretched flatly into an infinite and melancholy distance, but it looked to me sunlit and full of promise, like the setting of a fairy tale.

About noon we passed through a little plage on the Danube; it must have been Balaton, and there were groups of men and girls walking about in short bathing-suits. Nice their brown legs and arms looked and the hair of the girls in the fierce sun.

Pierre called out: 'Hungry?'

I said: 'Yes.'

But I grew uneasy again when we stopped for lunch at some little village of which I was never to know the unpronounceable name.

Through the open door of the restaurant the village looked bleak in the sunlight and pervaded with melancholy; flocks of geese, countless proud geese, strolled about; several old women sat on a long, low stone bench under a lime tree, on another bench two or three old men. The old women were really alarming. Their brown, austere faces looked as though they were carved out of some hard wood, the wrinkles cut deep. They wore voluminous dark skirts, handkerchiefs tied round their heads, and they sat quite silent, nearly motionless. How pitiless they would be, those ancient ones, to a sinner of their own sex – say a thief – how fiercely they would punish her. Brrrrr! Let us not think of these things.

Pierre said: 'What a life they must have, these people!'

I agreed: 'Dreadful!' looked away from the stone bench, drank my horrible coffee, and went outside. There was a girl, a maid of the inn perhaps, or a goose-girl, going in and out of the back door, carrying pails and tubs. She wore a white bodice so thin that one could plainly see the shape of her breasts, a dark skirt, her feet were bare, her head was small, set on a very long neck, her eyes slanted like Ishima's – I watched her with an extraordinary pleasure because she was so slim and young and finely drawn. And because I imagined that when she glanced at me her eyes had the expression of some proud, wild thing – say a young lioness – instead of the usual stupid antagonism of one female looking at another.

I said to Pierre: 'Oh, I do think that Hungarians can be lovely; they beat the Austrians hollow.'

He answered so indifferently: 'Another type,' that I began to argue.

'The Austrians are always trotting out their rotten old charm that everybody talks about. Hate people who do that. And they're fat and female and rusé and all the rest.'

'Oh!' said Pierre, 'and if you think that Hungarians aren't rusé, my dear, zut! – they are the most rusé of the lot, except the Poles.'

I insisted: 'In a different way. . . . Now look at that girl; isn't she lovely, lovely?'

'Un beau corps,' judged Pierre. 'Come on, Francine, let's get off if you are ready.'

I heard the apprehension in his voice and climbed into the car a little wearily. A grind . . . and we had left behind us that goose-girl out of a fairy tale against her background of blue distances quivering with heat.

I began to plan my triumphant return to Hungary with money to pay Pierre's debts. I saw myself sitting at the head of a long table handing little packets of notes to everyone concerned, with the stern countenance of a born business woman: 'Will you sign this, please?'

Then I must have slept, and when I woke I'd begun to feel as if the flight had lasted for days, as though I could not remember a time when I hadn't been sitting slightly cramped, a little sick, watching the country fly past and feeling the wind in my face.

Pierre turned and asked if I were tired or cold.

'No, I'm all right. . . . Are you going to drive? Well, don't go too fast . . . don't break our necks after all this.'

We left the flat country behind and there was a sheer drop one side of the road. The darkness crept up, the wind was cold. Now I was perfectly sure that it was all a dream and could wait calmly for the moment of waking.

We flitted silently like ghosts between two rows of dark trees. I strained my eyes to see into the frightening mystery of the woods at night, then slept again and the car had stopped when I woke.

'What is it?'

'The frontier . . . keep still. . . .'

An unexpected fuss at the frontier. There was a post. A number of men with rifles round a wood fire, an argument which became very loud and guttural. Our passports were produced: 'Kommission – Kurrier.'

'What is it, Pierre?'

He got out of the car without answering and followed one of the men into the shelter.

It was horrible waiting there in the night for what seemed hours, my eyes shut, wondering what jail would be like.

Then Pierre reappeared, still arguing, and got in beside me.

He muttered: 'Je m'en fiche, mon vieux,' and yelled to the chauffeur.

The car jumped forward like a spurred horse. I imagined

for one thrilling moment that we would be fired on, and the nape of my neck curled itself up. But when I looked back over my shoulder I saw the knot of men by the light of the fire looking after us as if they were puzzled.

'Frightened?'

'No, only of being sent back. What was it? Had they been told to stop us?'

'No, but nobody is supposed to pass. The frontier is shut, something has happened.'

I said: 'What can it be, I wonder,' without the slightest interest.

'Well,' said Pierre, 'here is Czechoslovakia, and goodbye Hungary!'

'Goodbye, Hungary!' Tears were in my eyes because I felt so tired, so deathly sick.

'You're awfully tired, aren't you, Frances?'

'A bit. I'd like to rest. Let's stop soon. Where will we spend the night?'

'At Presburg. We're nearly there.'

I huddled into a corner of the car and shut my eyes.

It was late when we found a room in the Jewish quarter of the town. All the good hotels were full; and in the hardest, narrowest bed I had ever imagined I lay down and was instantly asleep.

Next morning something of the exhilaration had come back. We went out to breakfast and to buy maps. It had been decided that we would go to Prague and there sell the car, and then . . .

'I want to go to Warsaw,' announced Pierre.

I said dismayed: 'Warsaw? but, my dear . . .'

The coffee was good, the rolls fresh; something in the air of the clean, German-looking little town had given me back my self-confidence.

I began to argue: 'We must go to London . . . in London . . .'

'Mon petit,' said Pierre, lighting his pipe, 'I don't believe in your friends helping us. I know how naïve you are. Wait, and you will see what your famous friends are worth. You will be roulée from the beginning to the end. Let's go to Warsaw. I believe I can arrange something there; Francine, do what I say for once.'

I told him obstinately that I did not like Poles. He shrugged his shoulders.

We found the car and Franzi waiting at the hotel.

'Off we go,' said Pierre, cheerfully, 'en route! Here's the brandy flask.'

The road was vastly better, but I had no comforting sensation of speed, of showing a clean pair of heels. Now we seemed to be crawling, slowly and painfully, ant-like, across a flat, grey and menacing country. I pictured that dreary flatness stretching on and on for miles to the north of Russia, and shivered.

I kept repeating to myself: 'I won't go and be buried in Poland. . . . I won't go. . . . I don't care. . . . I will not. . . .'

The wind was cold; it began to drizzle persistently.

'Pierre, we're off the road, I'm sure. That woman put us wrong. This is only a cattle-track.'

It was. And time was wasted going backwards. Pierre cursed violently all the while. He had begun to be in a fever of anxiety to reach Prague.

The walls of the bedroom where we slept that night were covered with lurid pictures of Austrian soldiers dragging hapless Czechoslovakians into captivity. In the restaurant downstairs a pretty girl, wearing a black cape lined with vivid purple, sat talking to two loutish youths. She smoked cigarette after cigarette with pretty movements of her hands and arms and watched us with bright blue, curious eyes.

We drank a still wine, sweetish, at dinner. It went to my head and again I could tell myself that my existence was a dream. After all it mattered very little where we went. Warsaw, London. . . . London, Warsaw. . . . Words! Quite without the tremendous significance I had given them.

It was still raining when we reached Prague at last. We made the dreary round of the hotels; they were all full, there were beds in the bathrooms of the Hotel du Passage; it was an hour before we discovered a room in a small hotel in a dark, narrow street.

Pierre began to discuss the sudden return of King Karl to Hungary. We heard the news at the Passage.

That was the trouble at the frontier, of course.

I said indifferently – I was lying down – 'Yes, probably.'

Karl – the Empress Zita – the Allies – Commission – the Whites – the Reds – Pierre himself . . . shadows! Marionnettes gesticulating on a badly lit stage, distracting me from the only reality in life . . . the terrible weight that bowed me down . . . the sickness that turned me cold and mounted up to cloud my brain.

Pierre advised me to have some strong coffee. He rang the bell and a short, fat waiter appeared who looked at me with that peculiar mixture of insolence, disdain, brutality and sentimentality only to be found amongst those of German extraction. Then he departed to fetch the coffee.

It was an odd place, that hotel, full of stone passages and things. I lay vaguely wondering why Prague reminded me of witches. . . . I read a book when I was a kid – *The Witch of Prague*. No. It reminded me of witches anyhow. Something dark, secret and grim.

'I think Prague is a rum place,' I told Pierre. 'What's that bell that keeps ringing next door?'

'A cabaret, cinema perhaps. . . . Listen, Frances, it's just the best of luck for us, that business of Karl. Nobody will worry about me just now. Ishima will be far too busy voting with the majority. . . . Sacré little Japanese!'

'Probably,' I agreed.

He asked me if I felt ill, suggested a doctor.

'A Czech doctor, my God!'

I pulled the sheets over my head. I only wanted to be left alone, I told him.

'Francine,' said he gently, 'don't be a little silly girl. The doctors are good here if you want one.'

He put the rug over me: 'Rest a bit while I go and see about the car. We'll dine at the Passage and find a place for dancing afterwards. Yes?'

I emerged from under the sheets to smile because his voice sounded so wistful, poor Pierre.

About six that evening I felt suddenly better and began to dress.

Because I noticed at lunch that the grand chic at Prague seemed to be to wear dead black I groped in the trunk for something similar, powdered carefully, rouged my mouth, painted a beauty spot under my left eye.

I was looking at the result when Pierre came in.

'My pretty Francine, wait a bit! I have something here to make you chic . . . but chic. . . .'

He felt into his pocket, took out a long case, handed it to me.

'Pierre!'

'Nice, hé?'

'Where did you get them?'

He did not answer.

I looked from the pearls to his dark, amused face, and then I blushed – blushed terribly all over my face and neck. I shut the case and gave it back to him and said: 'How much money have we got left?' And he answered without looking at me: 'Not much; the worst is this war-scare. Czechoslovakia is going to mobilize. It won't be so easy to sell the car. We must sell it before we can move. Never mind, Francine.'

I said: 'Never mind!' Then I took the case, opened it, clasped the pearls round my neck. 'If we're going the whole hog, let's go it. Come on.'

One has reactions, of course.

Difficult to go the whole hog, to leave respectability behind with an air, when one lies awake at four o'clock in the morning – thinking.

'Francine, don't cry . . . what is it?'

'Nothing. . . . Oh! do let me alone. . . .'

When he tried to comfort me I turned away. He had suddenly become a dark stranger who was dragging me over the edge of a precipice. . . .

It rained during the whole of the next week, and I spent most of the time in the hotel bedroom staring at the wallpaper. Towards evening I always felt better and would start to think with extraordinary lucidity of our future life in London or Paris – of unfortunate speculation and pearls – of a poker face and the affair of King Karl. . . .

One day at the end of our second week in Prague Pierre arrived with two tickets which he threw on the bed: 'There you are, to Liège, to London. . . . I sold it and did not get much; I tell you.' . . .

I spent an hour dressing for dinner that night. And it was a gay dinner.

'Isn't the chef d'orchestre like a penguin?'

'Yes, ask him to play the Saltimbanques Valse.'

'That old valse?'

'Well, I like it . . . ask him. . . . Listen, Pierre, have we still got the car?'

'Till tomorrow.'

'Well, go to the garage and get it. I'd like to drive like hell tonight. . . . Wouldn't you?'

He shrugged: 'Why not?'

Once more and for the last time we were flying between two lines of dark trees, tops dancing madly in the high wind.

'Faster! Faster! Make the damn thing go!'

We were doing a hundred.

I thought: he understands – began to choose the tree we would smash against and to scream with laughter at the old hag Fate because I was going to give her the slip.

'Get on! . . . get on! . . .'

We slowed up.

We were back at the hotel.

'You're drunk, Frances,' said Pierre severely.

I got out, stumbled, laughed stupidly – said: 'Goodbye! Poor old car,' gathered up the last remnants of my dignity to walk into the hotel. . . .

It was: 'Nach London!'

74 75 10 9 8 7 6 5 4 3 2 1